MW00930691

Murder and Passion in the Music City

Tami Ryan & Jim Cavanaugh

DEDICATION

This book is dedicated to all persons who have been touched by violent crime and all law enforcement officers who are dedicated to stopping violence and keeping everyone safe. It is also dedicated to everyone who has loved and lost and will love again.

CONTENTS

Murder and Passion in the Music City

ACKNOWLEDGMENTS

Copyright c 2023 by LM Authors, LLC

Tami Ryan and Jim Cavanaugh

Cover design by pro_ebooks

Front cover photograph by Tami Ryan

Book design by pro_ebooks

First edition

Thanks to our editor, Kathlyn Jones, who ensured that our book is well read. Without her, this dream would have been an uphill task. We are grateful.

Notice

Chapter One:
Satan's Henchman

There are two kinds of waiting lines, one where you want the line to hurry up, to get your coffee or movie ticket or food and the second, is where you want the line to slow down because you are waiting in fear for the night train to hell; that second one, that one, is death row.

It is hard to find a more foreboding place than death row. The whole atmosphere is otherworldly. It is both dank and cold while simultaneously being hot and sweaty. It has its own smell, as if fear had an odor. It has its own creepy sounds, and creepy silence. Even graveyards feel different, because there, death has passed by, and here, death has set the table and stands suffocatingly close.

Before a death sentence is carried out there is a death watch, a formal three-day period. It's important to maintain the security and control of a condemned offender and to maintain safe and orderly operations of the prison, therefore many procedures are in place. There are four cells adjacent to the execution chamber where the condemned inmate is watched constantly by a team of correctional officers who work 12-hour shifts. The offender is placed in one of the four cells. It has a bed with a mattress. There is also a shower, a stainless-steel sink and a toilet. It has a small window with a limited view of the grounds. Once the offender is placed on death watch, the items an inmate can have in the cell are limited; the visitation schedule differs from the rest of the prison. The media is not allowed to interview the offender during death watch. Supplies that are allowed are a tube of toothpaste, a toothbrush, a bar of soap and toilet tissue. One set of clothing and undergarments. Religious materials, Legal documents. One television outside the cell. Medication is prescribed by the facility's physician but is controlled by a corrections officer. One requested newspaper at a time in the cell. They have regular meals and the offender can request a special meal on the final day before the execution. Clean laundry. Appropriate clothing for the mortician. Mail privileges, except for packages. A telephone is available to make personal or legal calls which the warden approves. Only the

people on the offender's official visitation list are allowed to visit during death watch. The warden decides the number of visitors and the number of visits. All visits are non-contact until the final day at which time the warden can decide to grant a contact visit. Visits by spiritual advisor are under the same guidelines, and the warden can grant a visit prior to the execution. Only the prison chaplain can accompany the offender into the execution chamber if the offender requests. The condemned inmate's attorney can visit prior to the execution. Visiting hours are between 8:00 a.m. and 4:00 p.m., allowing one two-hour visit in the morning and one two-hour visit in the afternoon.

On the morning of the execution, the condemned man asked the corrections officer if he could make one final phone call. The officer says; "I'll have to get the warden's approval." He returned shortly and led the man from the cell a few steps away to a small antechamber. It contained a small table, a chair and a landline phone. The officer tells him to make his call as the officer remains nearby. The condemned man dials a number. After three rings the phone connects. The condemned man says, "Diablo, every dog has his day and my day is tomorrow." The person on the other end doesn't utter a word. He then hangs up. The condemned man is then led back to his cell.

Father Gunther arrived at the Riverbend Maximum Security Prison in Nashville at the appointed time. He made the trip many times before. He's Tennessee's prison chaplain for death row inmates. The priest walked into the main building using the security passes and waving at the guards, and walked directly to Warden Larry Mankowski's office ready to perform his duties. The warden greeted the priest warmly, they were friends. They had known each other for years. For many years, executions had been performed at midnight, but now different times were used to make it easier on staff and families. This execution was scheduled for 6:00 pm. Father Gunther and the Warden talked for a few minutes about the procedure and what was about to happen. The warden asked, "Is everything set? Do you need anything, Father? Are you ready to go?" The Priest answered,

"I'm ready warden." The warden and Father Gunther walked down the long hallway to the chamber on death row. The steel doors clanging behind them, the stillness of the air, the darkness of the moment always played on the priest's mind. He knew how serious the moment was in God's eyes, a man was about to lose his life, he was a child of God despite his crimes. As they entered the cell, the priest looked at the grizzled man seated on the bunk. He had administered to 100's of inmates, but this one was different. His presence was like a grip on your throat sending haunting vibrations straight to your heart. It shook the priest deeply but he forged ahead with his duties. "I'm Father Gunther and I am here to offer you The Last Rights before death. I understand you are Mr. Miller."

Miller said in a strong firm voice, "No thanks Father, I'm not interested in your Voodoo. I could care less about that bullshit."

Father Gunther responded, "Well, son, sometimes when people are about to meet their maker, they change their mind and want to offer a last prayer."

Miller replied in an angry tone, "I already told you Father I'm not interested. I want to go straight to Hell and I've wanted to go for a long time and I don't want you in my way." Father Gunther responded, "Alright son, I'll be praying for you anyway, good luck."

The priest turned on his heels like a whirling dervish fearing God had lost a soul. Walking out of the cell, he had the unnatural sensation of cold clammy fingers reaching after him as if he was escaping the grip of Satan.

The warden said, "Your last meal is on the way Miller." Just then one of the correction officers walked in with Miller's last meal. Miller smiled as the officer laid the meal on the table. It's fried chicken, boudin, collard greens, fried okra, two RC colas and a Moon Pie. Miller's favorites. He immediately started on the meal and ate voraciously like it's his last. When Miller finished his meal, he got a notice from the correction officer. "You've got 10 minutes Miller, and then we'll be going into the chamber." As Miller laid back on his bunk, thoughts raced through his head about everything that's gone on. His brother and how much he loved him. His parents, his childhood, and his time in the Military. He thought about growing up in South Pittsburg in East Tennessee, he thought about his life, his experience in the Navy being a welder and later an electrician. He thought about the mountains in East Tennessee, the cool mornings, the scenery, the trout streams and how much he loved being outside. Now, he was locked in this hell hole and it was coming to an end. But Miller was adamant, he wouldn't go out like a weasel. He would try to be strong; he was scared but wasn't going to let anybody know.

Just then, the correction officer and the warden arrived. The cell door opened, and Miller was walked down the hallway. The priest, standing a good distance behind but was still available. He knew that a man can change his mind when his doom is sealed. As they walked Miller to the execution room, he saw the glass windows where the witnesses were secured outside the chamber. They could see in but they couldn't hear what was going on unless the warden turns on the microphone. Miller saw the crowd. He knew some of the faces. He had no family there for him. He saw his attorney who he felt betrayed by. He saw the reporters who reported his case on the news. He hated them passionately as well. The truth is, the only person Miller ever loved was his brother. *The whole human race was a cesspool* he thought. Good Riddance. The corrections officer laid him on the gurney and strapped him in. The Doctor inserted the IV that would administer the drugs to his arm carefully and connected the tubes. The spectators outside were silent as they observed the morbid process. They couldn't hear anything but they could watch as the night drew the curtain over Miller's life. They could see Miller's countenance, The warden's stoicism. They could feel the gravity of the situation. One reporter thought, *when a life is about to be lost the air is thick with the hurry of spirits looking to claim a soul.* He knew that every day we see tragedies with multiple lives lost, but it never feels this heavy. *Why?* His thoughts took him back to a writing in the ancient Jewish Holy Book called "The Talmud" that says, if you save one life you save the world. He wondered if it works the other way. *If you take one life, do you lose the world?*

The reporters assembled as witnesses included a who's who of the Nashville media. There was Frank Lee of the ABC affiliate, Deb Manek of NBC, Herbie Johnson from the Tennessean and Al Scarborough from FOX News. The CBS reporter was Heather Milo. The big news radio was Hal Hedgepath. Everything went quiet for a moment. The witnesses saw the warden and the condemned man now alone in the death chamber talking. The microphone was not on so they couldn't hear what was being said but the conversation lasted for a few minutes. Then the warden stepped out of the room. They turned on the microphone. Miller was left alone on the gurney staring at the ceiling. The warden's voice came over the loud speaker for Miller and the spectators to hear. The warden said, "OK lieutenant, administer the drugs."

Miller looked at the small crowd assembled outside the glass straining against the straps, the veins in his neck were bulging and popping. Screaming and spitting as he yelled, "I made an appointment for y'all at the gates of Hell, and it's gonna be sooner than you think!" He then laughs manically, the laugh of a madman. The spectators could feel an uncomfortable chill fill the room.

The next moment the drip from the IV bag was visible and Miller turned his head rapidly side to side in a blank-eyed death dance. He was trying to see everything in an ocean of nothing. Looking, looking until he was engulfed in the final abyss. Reporters knew that the first drug administered puts the inmate to sleep and the second drip was to cause death. There was not much visible to watch. There was a little twitching of his body. They strained to see his face but there were no clues now that he was so still. In a few minutes, the door opened, the warden and a physician came in. The warden stepped back, the physician then put his stethoscope on Miller's chest, he touched his neck, he turned to the warden and pronounced him deceased.

Chapter Two:
An Insufferable Union-13 Years Earlier

Lonnie and Jo-Sue lived in a neighborhood of Nashville called Hermitage, a pool of quiet in the otherwise brass and brash of the Music City. Many families have lived there for years. They raised children and grandchildren; they had Christmas parties and cook-outs. They also had proms and weddings. A true slice of Americana. Lonnie and Jo-Sue have lived there for nine years, having bought their house shortly after getting married. Lonnie works at the Nissan plant in Smyrna on the day shift, while Jo-Sue was a part-time bank teller in Donelson. They have no children, just a dog. A yappy little yorkie that was Jo-Sue's baby. She named him Pickles. Lonnie hated that dog and the dog knew it. The second Lonnie walked in the house Pickles started in, and the constant yapping lighted a smoldering glow of exasperation in Lonnie's eyes. All Lonnie desired was some peace and quiet after a hard day's work. Jo-Sue would allow Pickles to bark at Lonnie for several minutes before picking him up and quieting him down. She knew it irritated Lonnie and she did her best to irritate him at all times. Pickles was an extension of Jo-Sue and every day when he got home, he wanted to grab Pickles by the throat and toss him in a dumpster. It was always like a tag team wrestling event between Jo-Sue and Pickles. If one wasn't yapping at him the other one was. Living with Jo-Sue was like having Syphilis, Small pox and Bloomer Crickets all at the same time.

On the other hand, Pickles did keep Jo-Sue busy and out of Lonnie's hair for the most part. Their marriage had deteriorated several years ago. Jo-Sue had been so kind and loving when Lonnie first met her. She was extremely sweet and he loved being with her. After a few years, she started changing and getting saltier; berating him at every turn. Jo-Sue was a shrew and a harpy, and she belittles Lonnie at every chance that she can. Nothing was good enough for her. No amount of money was enough. Lonnie made good money and Jo-Sue got a part-time job at a bank for something to do. It was her money to spend how she pleased and it all went to Pickles. Now they absolutely disgust each other. When Lonnie got home from work, he made himself as small as possible. He didn't stay out in the bars until late and he didn't spend money foolishly, he only took a couple of beers to relax for a few minutes after work, or maybe watched a ball game. That's it. Jo-Sue would start on him as soon as he walked in the door.

"You were supposed to clean out the garage two days ago. You didn't take the trash out this morning and now it's going to sit and stink for another week. The lawn needs to be mowed.

I told you my car is making a noise four days ago. All you ever want to do is sit and drink beer. Maybe you could get your lazy ass up and do something. I don't think I should have to do EVERYTHING around here. You're lucky I even bother to make you dinner. Maybe I'll stop making dinner until you get all your stuff done," Jo-Sue said.

It went on and on. It seemed like it would never end. Lonnie sat and drank his beer. He learned a long time ago that when Jo-Sue gets like this, it was best to let her rant and cuss and get it over with. Lonnie finished his two beers, got up and went outside. He went to start on the garage. Basically, he went to the garage to get away from Jo-Sue. Whenever any neighbors were around or walking by, Jo-Sue would bring out her alter ego. That Jo-Sue was as sweet and kind as she could be. That side of her was the woman he married. If any neighbor had an issue, whether they were sick, or in the hospital or had a death in the family, Jo-Sue was right there with a great dinner making sure they were taken care of. She would even offer to go to the store for them. She would do whatever she could do to help them out. He missed that Jo-Sue but he knew this Jo-Sue was putting on an act. The neighbors knew it as well and played along. He doesn't know what happened. He can't say with exact timing when it all changed. Their marriage died and he doesn't know why. It's now an angry bitter relationship that Lonnie felt forced to endure. Whenever Jo-Sue would start in, her sandpaper tongue would scold him to a fine finish. They didn't have a ton of money and Lonnie knew if he divorced her, she would want every single thing they have, every dime that is saved and would expect

Lonnie to give her money every month. Yes, Lonnie would literally have nothing. He often felt it would be worth it but he wasn't strong enough at this point to start any proceedings.

Jo-sue would not divorce Lonnie because she knew how good she had it. She worked a few hours a week for something to do and Lonnie's money supported them 100%. She knew what side her bread was buttered. If she had to endure him to make sure she got what she wanted, so be it. Twice a year, in the Spring and the Fall, their neighborhood would have a block party. In the Spring to celebrate the upcoming great weather and again in the Fall to say good-bye to the great weather. There was a small park at the end of the main street and that's where they had the festival. Everybody brought a dish to pass and their own dishes, chairs, and drinks. Someone had a great Bluetooth speaker and all sorts of music was playing throughout the party. Plenty of playground equipment was there for the kids. There was also a covered pavilion in case it was raining and plenty of picnic tables to accommodate everyone. Usually, the entire neighborhood showed up at some point. About 200 people would come and go throughout the day. The block party was coming up this weekend and Jo-Sue was busy getting lots of food ready to take. She was a great cook and the neighbors were always interested to see what she was going to bring. The neighborhood denizens knew how fake Jo-Sue was; that she pretended to like or care about everybody. She was always determined to outshine anybody and if that meant doing something nice, she would suffer through to get the accolades she felt she deserved. Lonnie knew Jo-Sue really didn't care much for any of the neighbors, but she always wanted to be in the limelight at party time, so she would put on her fake, sweet persona and flits around like a fancy butterfly. The only thing Lonnie had to do was make sure he had his Pabst Blue Ribbon to take. Jo-Sue told him many times he was too stupid to help. Lonnie was fine with that since she would bitch at him that he never does anything right. *What a miserable creature,* Lonnie thought.

About halfway through the party on Saturday night, Jo-Sue had too much to drink. She was getting loud, which was what she always does. In front of everybody she started in on Lonnie. She made snide nasty remarks, dug at Lonnie and then laughed and said she was just joking. It went on and on. She remarked haughtily how bad he was in bed and that she had to always take the lights out just to have sex with him. He couldn't satisfy a blow-up doll. The neighbors were clearly uncomfortable with this. They grew silent and someone in the crowd had the good grace to change the subject. As Lonnie turned to get out of this embarrassing situation, he made eye contact with a lady down the street, named Delores Swenson. Everyone heard what Jo-Sue said and Delores's heart went out to Lonnie. He was an incredibly quiet man and Delores found him to be kind and gentle from what she knew about him. She saw him frequently in the neighborhood. If she drove by and he's out he would wave. If she's out walking, he would always say hi. Just a very keep to himself kind of guy. "I heard all that and nobody should be that cruel," she said to Lonnie. "Well, she hates me. She makes Cruella Deville look like Mother Teresa," Lonnie replied. They shared a laugh.

Delores continued, "My ex was like that. He would say very vile things to me and about me that were not true. That is why he is my ex. You can't imagine how much better your life gets when you remove the negative force that is holding you down. I hope you can get away from Jo-Sue someday. She has a wicked tongue that could slice steel. Do you want to come to my place and have a drink? We can sit out front and get away from the madness and let things die down." Lonnie agreed.

They went to Delores house and sat on the front step and had a drink. Lonnie opened up to Delores about his life with Jo-Sue, how it started out great and somewhere in the middle how it had turned sour. Lonnie felt trapped. He doesn't know why he stayed. They had no kids to contend with. Probably because he has been so beaten down, and lacked the energy to get up and fight. The night was getting chilly so they went inside and sat at the kitchen table. Lonnie felt like he finally found someone who listened and understood him. As he poured his heart out, Delores just sat and listened intently. They had a couple more drinks. Delores could sympathize with Lonnie since her ex-husband had been the same way. She talked about her transformation after her divorce. "Yes, getting a divorce is hard. Especially when one person is as nasty and as negative as my ex and Jo-Sue. But in the end, you'll be free and your life will be amazing. You just have to find the right time for you to take the plunge. You'll know when that is," she said. After sitting and talking for a couple of hours, Delores decided that Lonnie was a good man. A hard-working man that was being beaten down by a cloven-hoofed devil of a woman. Delores kind of knew Jo-Sue. They spoke every once in a while. She was nice enough to the neighbors but everyone knew how she treated Lonnie and nobody in the neighborhood really liked her. She had an arrogant and nasty disposition and she didn't always save all of her nastiness for Lonnie.

Over the next several months, Lonnie would go down to Delores' house and they would sit and have drinks and talk. They talked about everything and nothing. Jo-Sue knew Lonnie would take a walk in the nice evening summer air. She was glad he did. He was gone and away from her, which was how she preferred it. She wasn't worried about Lonnie. Nobody in their right mind would want anything to do with him.

Lonnie and Delores had become quite good friends. They laughed and joked, and truly enjoyed each other's company. They stayed in the house. Delores didn't want there to be any reason for anybody to go back and tell Jo-sue that Lonnie was at her house. They were just friends, but when the rumor mills get working it would work overtime on this. Lonnie didn't care, but he knew if any sort of rumor got out about him and Delores, Jo-sue would make her life a living hell and Lonnie liked Delores enough to make sure that didn't happen. In fact, Lonnie wondered what his life would be like if he was married to Delores. She was sweet, kind, funny and sympathetic to his life. But Jo-Sue started out that way and now she had become a harridan. Lonnie always kept his guard up when around Delores. After about 5 months, Lonnie and Delores had drawn closer. They became extremely comfortable around each other and truly enjoyed each other's company. One night, they were on her back deck. It was quiet, away from any prying eyes. They had the lights off so nobody could see anything. Not that they were doing anything, but nosey neighbors were a danger. They were having their drinks and talking; their usual time together. Delores couldn't help herself. She got up off her chair, went over to Lonnie, leaned down and kissed him. Lonnie was caught off guard. He had been thinking about this for months. He didn't know how Delores felt about him and he certainly wasn't going to make any move to jeopardize their friendship. But here she was leaning over him and kissing him. He was kissing her back. He could not believe this was happening. He was so surprised, so he stopped kissing her and stood up.

"Oh Lonnie, I am so sorry, I couldn't help myself. It's been months and months of us being together and I just had to kiss you. I hope you are not mad," Delores said. Before she could continue Lonnie walked over to her, grabbed her and started kissing her. Deeply, madly, lovingly kissing her. She felt wonderful in his arms. She kissed him back with such intensity she thought she was going to faint. They stood there for what seemed like an eternity hugging and kissing. When they finally stopped, Lonnie says, "I better go. This was incredible but for now I better go." "I'm sorry Lonnie, I didn't mean to make you uncomfortable," Delores replied. "Delores, you do NOT need to worry. It was incredible and I have been thinking about this for months. You are a much braver person than I to take the first step and I am excited that you did. But for tonight, I think I better go so we can both cool down and think about what is going to happen in the future," Lonnie said. Delores agreed. They shared another deep kiss on her deck and Lonnie headed home. He was hoping his erection would subside before getting home. *Oh yeah*, he mused, *all he had to do was think about Jo-Sue and his erection would instantly disappear, so no problem.*

A couple of days later when Lonnie was hanging out with Delores, they were again on her deck having drinks. They discussed what happened the last time and how excited they both were. They were sitting together on a deck chaise. Lonnie's arm was around Delores and they were holding hands. Their conversation turned to how much they have grown to truly and deeply care for each other and that maybe they could have a future together. Sitting quietly together, enjoying each other's company. Suddenly Delores stood and pulled Lonnie up to stand, then she took off his belt. She helped him off with his pants. "Wait a minute, what are you doing?" Lonnie said. "What?" she says. "Delores we are outside on your deck," Lonnie said. "So? Nobody can see us. It'll be fine. Please just relax," Delores responded. She had Lonnie sit back down on the chaise. She knelt between his legs, then she leaned in and started kissing him again while she caressed him between his legs. Together they felt rivers of fire coursing through their bodies. Lonnie couldn't believe this. He hadn't had sex in years. He would masturbate every once in a while, but that doesn't count. Now Delores, this kind, gentle, loving woman who had been his confident for months had his pants down and was playing with him. He was kissing her back. When he tried to move, she made a motion to just stay still, stay seated and enjoy. Delores continued to caress him very softly and slowly. Without warning, she put her mouth on him. He was so hard that it hurt. She wasted no time. She had him full in her mouth. He tried to hold back. He tried to hang on but he couldn't. This whole scene was so erotic and sexy. This had never happened to him and he couldn't help himself. He exploded, it was incredible, it was so intense he couldn't breathe. She was prepared because she knew Lonnie hadn't been satisfied in years. She stood up to get a drink of water and sat on the chair next to Lonnie. He wasn't saying or doing anything. He just sat there trying to recover from what just happened. Once he was completely recovered, he wanted to reciprocate the enjoyment to Delores. "No, not tonight," she said. Lonnie asked why not. Delores told him that, that was for him. That was for him being the good man she knew he was. He has been tortured long enough and she wanted him to know that there was someone who saw that and appreciated him. She told him there will be plenty of opportunity to continue but for now, it's all about him. Lonnie was stunned, this came out of the blue. He had wanted to be with Delores for months now but didn't know how to proceed since he was married. He did not want her to think he was a jerk for messing around on his wife. Delores knew that's how Lonnie was. Even though his wife clearly hated him, he was still a married man and he wanted to stick to that. Now everything was thrown into a blender and turned on high. Regardless, he was on cloud 9. He adored Delores and wanted to be around her and with her. Lonnie put his pants back on, and they talked for a little while longer. Lonnie had to go. He was very diligent about not adding any extra time to his "walk" so it doesn't raise any suspicions. They stood on Delores' back deck and embraced, kissed each other so intently and deeply. Lonnie has never been kissed like this by Jo-Sue. This was gentle, loving, sensual, delicate and meaningful. What would he do? He wanted this relationship with Delores. How long would she be willing to have an affair with him before having the guts to divorce Jo-Sue? Is he strong enough to divorce Jo-Sue? With Delores in his corner, he believed he could. He had to start figuring things out. He's got to go talk to an attorney about his options. But for now, his time with Delores was going to be amazing and he couldn't wait to make love to her. Making love properly. With gentleness and kindness. The thought of that was going to drive him crazy until it happened. He still had to be very careful around Jo-Sue. He had to maintain his consistent behavior as not to give her a reason to be suspicious. Lonnie quickly realized Jo-Sue could give two shits about where he was or where he went. Whenever he came home from his "walk", he would see her sitting on the couch wrapped up with Pickles watching one of her 100's of reality shows; ignoring him completely. He would go take a shower and go to bed with Jo-Sue neither caring if he was there or not.

Lonnie's affair with Delores was incredible. They were very careful about their timing. Lonnie wanted to be there every night, but Delores agreed with him that for now, they needed to be cautious. They took advantage of every moment they had. Their love making was incredible to Lonnie. Delores welcomed him in and he felt wanted. He knew she wanted him. Whenever he left Delores' house, he felt like he was leaving the comfort of his mother's warm embrace and now he was walking back into a burning ring of fire that was his daily life.

Delores wondered how much longer she was going to be able to keep up this affair. She loved Lonnie. She wanted to spend the rest of her life with him. They kept talking about divorce but it never seemed to go anywhere. *I have Lonnie's back*, she thought. And if Jo-Sue takes everything, let her take it. It's only stuff. We would have each other and that's what's most important. Something's got to give. With Lonnie being gone for the weekend, it gave Delores enough time to think about her future. She decided that when Lonnie got back, she was going to come right and tell him. *It's me or Jo-Sue. You decide right now. I'm not living like this any longer.* She would let the chips fall where they may.

Lonnie was excited about his upcoming fishing trip. He goes twice a year to Florence, Alabama and stays with his brother-in-law, Barry, who was married to Jo-Sue's sister, Eleanor. Lonnie stayed for the weekend and Eleanor went to Hermitage to spend the weekend with Jo-Sue. Lonnie thoroughly enjoyed these trips. His brother-in-law was aware of the situation. There was no love lost between Jo-Sue and Barry, and he welcomed Lonnie with no angst or accusations regarding his marriage to Jo-Sue. But this year Lonnie was torn. He relished his fishing trips but leaving Delores for a few days was hurting his heart. But it was only for a couple of nights and Delores would be on his mind always. She had become the light and warmth for his soul. He genuinely loved this woman and when he got back from this fishing trip, he was going to tell her that things were going to change dramatically and they were going to be together. He didn't want to lose Delores and he could no longer live with Jo-sue. This fishing trip was the calm before the storm. And what a storm it would be!

Chapter Three:
The Developing Fortress of a Woman

Tomi Bardsley grew up in a small town in upstate, New York. Hamilton, New York. A small farming community of 7,000 people. There were 125 kids in her graduating class. She was not one of the popular ones but she wasn't a loner either. Being very middle of the road. She was nice to everyone and not judging anybody. Her home life taught her to be kind because you just don't know what people are going through. She was one of those people who went through a lot. Being one of six, number three in line. Her parents divorced when she was five and her dad had no interest in being a parent. She had an abusive step-dad and a mother who didn't protect her kids from the emotional and verbal abuse. She had been taught that what goes on at home, stays at home. Only one of her friends was aware of how her home life was and that was Gemma Hughes. Tomi and Gemma met at the Broad Street diner where they both waitressed. They became instant friends. Neither Tomi or Gemma was into after school activities. Tomi tried to spend as much time at Gemma's since it was calmer than her own home. This kept her out of the line of fire from her step-dad. Gemma's parents never seemed to mind that Tomi was at their place. Tomi had a sneaky suspicion that Gemma's parents were aware of her home life and let her seek refuge whenever she needed it. She never considered Hamilton her home. She lived in a house with seven other people. If she were to ever go back, she would not say she was going home rather she would say she was going to Hamilton, NY. Gemma was ready to get out of Hamilton as well so they both decided to work and save as much money as they could to get out as soon as they graduated. Gemma's path took her to Nashville where, hopefully, her singing career would take off. Gemma had an amazing voice and Tomi just knew she would be successful. Tomi always had an adventurous spirit and it was hard for her to sit still. She had wanted to be a reporter and when she turned 18, she happily left her life in upstate. She was saying goodbye to Hamilton and had no plans to ever return. There was nothing in Hamilton for her so she felt no reason to ever go back.

Gemma wanted Tomi to come to Nashville with her but Tomi was able to secure a job as a cub television reporter covering New Jersey crime for a Local NYC News station. She covered the Police and Fire Departments in Newark which was a busy beat. It wasn't long before she met Joel Williams, a firefighter, whom she interviewed about an arson fire. In her initial interview, she couldn't really tell what he looked like since he was covered in soot and sweat, yet he flashed her the most

 beautiful smile and she couldn't help but fall in love with him that very second.   Another firefighter had come over and handed him a bottle of water. Joel took a long drink and then washed his face. His looks took her breath away. She had never seen someone so handsome. She was struggling to form the words to start her interview and Joel had sensed it.

Joel: "Miss, did you want to do an interview?"

Tomi: "Uh, Oh, What? Of course, the interview. So sorry.

Are you able to tell immediately whether or not this is arson?"

Joel: "Sometimes it's pretty easy to pick up, other times it takes an inspection."

Tomi: "Oh OK. What is your thought on this particular fire?"

Joel: "It's my job to put them out and I let the Arson Squad do their job. Would you mind telling me your name?"

Tomi hesitates. "It's Tomi Bardsley."

Joel: "Well Tomi Bardsley, my truck company is finished here and we are going back to the station, then I am done for the day. If you'd like to go to dinner, we can discuss fires over a glass of wine."

Tomi, still struck by his looks, just stared at him.

Joel: "Ms. Bardsley? Dinner?"

Tomi: "Oh, excuse me. Yes, sure, of course dinner. I would enjoy that."

Joel: "I can pick you up or we can meet. It is your choice."

Tomi: "I will meet you at Luigi's. How about 7:00 p.m."

Joel: "Perfect, see you then."

Their relationship started at that moment. Joel had been a fire fighter for eight years. His grandfather and his father had both been Newark firefighters, so it just seemed natural for him to follow in their footsteps. Joel spent years hanging out at the fire station with his two brothers and knew every inch of the building. He loved hearing the bell alerting them to a fire and watching the firefighters race to get ready. Joel was assigned to 9 Truck, a hook and ladder company on Avon Avenue in Newark's Central Ward. It was the second busiest truck company in New Jersey; the busiest was 5 Truck on Belmont Avenue, the next district over. The firehouse at Avon Avenue and 13th Street housed 9 truck, Engine 18 and the Chief of the Fourth Battalion. The Chief rode in an SUV the firefighters called a "Gig", he had a driver as well. Each Truck Company had 4 Firefighters and a Captain at full strength. A driver, a Tiller man who drove the rear wheels and two others. But they were rarely at full strength. More often it was 3 & 1 because of injuries and details. When it got down to 2 firefighters, they would ask for a detailed fireman from a slower firehouse.

Within six months Joel and Tomi moved in together and after two years they had finally gotten engaged. When neither were working, they loved going to the Jersey Shore spending as much time at the beach as they could. They spent hours talking about their future. Getting a house, kids, etc. Joel wanted at least four. Tomi was a little overwhelmed by that but she knew Joel would be an amazing dad and a great parent partner. She spent very little time worrying about the number of kids they would have because that was a few years down the road. For now, her goal was to be Joel's wife and start this new amazing life together.

Life was perfect. Becoming Joel's future wife was exactly what she wanted. It had become a far cry from the upbringing of always feeling sad and alone. Tomi and Joel both understood the demands of their careers and accepted and appreciated the time together when they got it.

Joel knew what Tomi liked; he knew what she needed. They never wasted a minute of their time together. Joel knew every inch of Tomi's body and knew every sensitive part. Their lovemaking seemed to last for hours. The way he caressed her nipples, soft and tender yet firm enough for her to feel it in her stomach. Kissing his way down her body, stopping and waiting for her to catch her breath. Ever so lightly caressing her. Every once in a while, licking her gently. He knew exactly when the time was right and he would put his whole mouth on her and bring her to extreme orgasms, pressing and licking until she begged him to stop. He would lay there and watch her shutter as her orgasm subsided. When she recovered, it was Joel's turn. Tomi also knew every inch of Joel's sensitive spots. When she went down on him, she knew he loved the slow movement. Her tongue licking the tip of him before putting him in her mouth. She would lick the shaft all the way down to the base and back up. Repeating that over and over. She knew when he was ready and she would climb on top of him and ride him until he exploded. They were compatible in every sense and it showed in their lovemaking.

Two months after their engagement, Tomi got called to report on a major fire. It involved 9 truck which was Joel's truck. Going to watch him do his job was always exciting for Tomi even when she was there covering the story. This was a huge fire in the industrial district near Port Newark. It had already gone to four alarms. A one-alarm fire involves multiple engines, and hook and ladder companies and that increases exponentially as the alarms increased. A four-alarm fire can have 12 to 16

engine companies, six to eight ladder companies, Battalion Chiefs, Deputy Chiefs, Rescue companies and tactical units with more man power. It's a large event and Tomi was right in the middle of it and she knew Joel was too. About 45 minutes after Tomi's arrival with the fire still burning pretty good there was a loud explosion at the scene. You could tell the whole atmosphere had changed. As fire fighters ran around, she heard them yelling "Get rescue 2 in here! There's been a backdraft explosion!" Whatever it was, it was awful loud. It shook the rafters and all the fire fighters reacted. Now they were moving even faster than they were before fighting the fire. Trying to get more and more people rushing towards the scene. It looked like one of the industrial buildings had collapsed in the center and there was a ton of frantic activity.

Tomi and the other news crews on the scene were filming this. It was very, very dramatic footage. As fire fighters moved by, Tomi heard someone yell, "9 Truck is trapped in the collapse after the backdraft! Get Rescue 2 in here! Get Heavy Rescue. Get more men in here, we need to pull these men out!" Tomi's heart sank to her stomach. 9 Truck was Joel's company. *Are they all trapped, just a few, is Joel among them, is he out?* She had no idea. She was waiting and watching intently at all the

frantic movement near the collapsed building. She saw more fire fighters going in and out constantly. The building was still on fire. Smoke was pouring out, Men yelling, radios were crackling. The news crews were all positioning to get the best shots. In the distance with a camera, she could see them dragging a fire fighter out of the rubble. He was quickly thrown on a stretcher, rushed off to the side where paramedics worked on him. They stripped off his helmet and worked on his chest. She saw an ambulance pull in. The fire fighters put the man in the ambulance and it sped away. *Oh My God* she thinks, *could that be Joel?* There was more digging, more officers moving around, and in a few minutes, she spotted the white helmet. That was the Battalion Chief. If she could just get to him, she might be able to find out what's going on.

Minutes passed and frantic activity at the scene continued. Soon, they pulled another fire fighter from the rubble. They moved him to the side; paramedics worked on him as well. He was put in the back of a second ambulance and raced off. That's two fire fighters pulled out. *Are they both from 9 Truck?* She wondered. *Could one of them be Joel?* She hoped the Battalion Chief would come closer; he'll have the answers. Minutes continued to tick by. She was getting more worried. Nothing was happening, things seemed to slow down at the scene of the explosion. Everybody seemed to be walking slower now. Something had changed. The Battalion Chief's face blackened with soot, and drained of his last drip of energy walked slowly towards Tomi. In a voice low and slow that could barely be heard over the surrounding racket he says, "I am so sorry Tomi." Before he could finish his sentence, Tomi collapsed screaming. The Battalion Chief was able to catch her before she hit the ground. He carried her to the nearest ambulance. The love of her life was gone. The man who had her heart and soul. The man who was ingrained in every fiber of her being. The man who took her breath away after three years of being together was snatched away from her in a blink of an eye. She always knew that was a possibility but the longer they were together and every time he came home, it just seemed like a distant possibility. Her Joel was gone.

The funeral was four days later at the Sacred Heart Church in Newark. Funerals for fire fighters were spectacles in themselves. When firefighters, unfettered by fear, walk into hells mouth to fight the flames and are lost, citizens know these are a special breed. Consequently, they turned out in droves to line the sidewalks for the final salute. When firefighters in the prime of life pay the ultimate sacrifice, it leaves everyone crushed to their souls. They know and remember other fire fighters and their families that have gone

through this before. A high funeral mass will be celebrated in the church. It was packed with Joel's family and of course, Tomi in the front row. The church was a sea of fire fighters all in their dress blues. The white hats of the Chiefs could be seen. All the fire fighters from 9 Truck and Engine 18 which was in the same house were located in the front pews of the church and as pallbearers for Joel. Out in front of the church was Engine 18 and 9 Truck. The engine was stripped of its hoses on the top because that is where Joel's casket would go. A hearse never carried a fire fighter killed in the line of duty. It was always a fire apparatus. During the course of the funeral mass, the fire bell that had been mounted on 9 truck was removed and put in the church and as the priest read the prayers for Joel, fire fighters in white gloves rang the bell 9 times for 9 Truck. When the mass was over, the casket was put on the shoulders of the pallbearers, taken down the aisle and down the marble steps outside of the church and hoisted to the top of Engine 18. Draped in black, 18 would follow 9 Truck all the way to the cemetery. The casket could not be put on the hook and ladder company because the ladders on the back took up all the room. The procession to the cemetery began with citizens lined on both sides of the streets. Newark motorcycles officers leading the way. Police cars were behind them, then the fourth Battalion Chief, 9 Truck and Engine 18 carrying Joel.

Then, Joel's family and Tomi in a limo. Also, there was a long line of fire companies from Newark. Engines and Hook and Ladders, Rescue Squads, Tactical Fire department vehicles stretched for 15 blocks. Fire apparatus from the surrounding communities were also present and that increased the procession. People along the sidewalks would never see this many fire trucks at one time unless the city was burning down. It seemed like it would never end. At the entrance to the cemetery, two Hook and Ladder companies extended their aerial ladders and hung a gigantic American Flag between them, so that when Engine 18 carrying Joel's body entered the cemetery, Joel and his family and Tomi would have to drive under the flag.

When they arrived at the cemetery, the Newark police honor guard was prepared and as Joel's casket was laid into the ground and the prayers were said, the police honor guard gave Joel a 21-gun salute. Fire Companies wailed their sirens, salutes were given, and prayers were said. Joel's parents wanted Tomi to take the folded American Flag that had draped Joel's casket. She tried to refuse but they insisted it was what Joel would have wanted. She almost fainted when the Chief of the Fire Department handed it to her but she held on.

The funeral was over for Joel, the burial ceremony was finished but not the pain and agony that was left for the fire fighters, Joel's family and especially for Tomi.

Losing Joel was more than she could bare. Tomi felt like she was never going to recover, her life as she knew it was over and had no idea where to turn or how to move on. It took her months of grieving and anger and she finally came to the realization that Joel would not want her to live like this. She couldn't bear to pack up Joel's things. She hadn't moved a thing since he died. Sleeping in his shirts until his smell dissipated, and then she would grab another one and start the process all over. Joel's family convinced her to let them come in and pack his things up so she could start to move forward. Coming home after his things were gone made it final. Joel was gone, her future was gone. The life she had planned with this amazing man was gone. They loved life and grabbed it with both hands and Joel would be disappointed if she continued down this path. Staying in Newark was just too painful. She set out to find somewhere that had a slower pace. Where hopefully she could put the devastation of Joel's death behind her. Where exactly, she didn't know.

Several weeks after Joel died, her best friend Gemma, urged her to move to Nashville for a whole new life out of the Northeast. Tomi had always wanted to go to Nashville and see Gemma and to take in the excitement and great country music. It was far enough from Newark to do just that. She reached out to the local television channels to see if they had any need for a night time reporter and Channel 4 decided to give her a chance. Two months later, she was packed up and heading south.

It didn't take her long to settle in. She was intrigued when she saw the river of neon in downtown Nashville. The bars in Nashville are located on Lower Broadway and these honky-tonks play music 24/7. On the weekends, Broadway was blocked off from traffic at night, so you could walk to and from the bars and be safe. There was Tootsie's Orchid Lounge, Roberts Western World, Layla's, The Stage, Jason Aldean's Rooftop Kitchen & Bar, Luke Bryant's 32 Bridge, Dierks Bentley's Whiskey Row, Miranda Lambert's Casa Rosa, Alan Jackson's AJ's Good Time Bar, John Rich's Redneck Riviera, Kid Rock's Honky-Tonk and Florida Georgia Line's FGL House. Just some of the celebrity bars. Of course, there were the favorite little hole in the wall places like Legends Corner and Second Fiddle. There are several rooftop bars where you have a bird's eye view of everything going on. The pulsating flow of the crowd and the music emanating from every crevasse caused her to taste the energy and tingle with excitement. It gave one the feeling that, at this place, life was happening more than at any other. She loved going to Robert's Western World and the Stage to listen to Gemma. She sang at The Local a lot. That was

farther up the street on West End Avenue. Again, a little place with a great atmosphere. Gemma was an amazing singer, and the times Tomi was able to spend with her gave her a sense of comfort that she desperately needed. It gave her time to recover. She was drawn in by the eclectic atmosphere that downtown Nashville provided. Great sounds and amazing people watching. The first time she walked into Robert's to listen to Gemma, she was struck at how quaint it was. You'd think it was this huge venue but it was far from it. The stage was on the left side right when you walked in the door. A small dance floor. A few tables up front. Some high tops tables on the left side and a small bar on the right. The wall on the left side had shelves and shelves of cowboy boots. The place was packed with locals and tourists dancing and having a fabulous time. The vibe in there was intense and you couldn't help but free fall into a great time. Every 30 minutes a new bachelorette party walked in the door. Bathed in fun, they smiled, danced and laughed their way to the bar. Not a care in the world. Their happiness was infectious as they lit the dim bar with their smiles. Tomi couldn't help but think that for this brief shining moment, these girls were making Nashville a better place.

Since she had moved to Nashville things had been pretty quiet and there was not much happenings to report on. She was OK with that at first, trying to get her mind and heart straight.

After a while, she was ready to get back to life and back to work. She wanted a slower pace but was so used to the constant reporting on crime in Newark that she had to adjust to her new surroundings. It didn't take long for things to change dramatically.

Chapter Four:
The Scales of Justice are Tipped

Judge John Moran lived in the Belle Meade section of Nashville. Belle Meade was the richest city in the area and one of the top richest cities in America. It was its own little municipality within Metropolitan Nashville. It was incredibly unique; it had a small police force. Of course, major crimes in Belle Meade were handled by the Nashville Metro Police detectives. But most things in this quiet community were handled by the Belle Meade police force. It did not have its own fire department. That was also handled by the Nashville Metropolitan Fire Department. So, it was a wealthy enclave just off West End Avenue and close to downtown Nashville. Between the city of Belle Meade and downtown Nashville was Vanderbilt University where Judge John Moran had matriculated both as an undergraduate and to its prestigious Law School. Judge Moran was born to wealthy parents. His father was a Defense Attorney who practiced injury law for years and was extremely wealthy. When he passed away a few years ago, he left John a fortune. John lived on the richest street in Belle Meade, Chickering, in a very large and beautiful mansion. He had a wife named Betsy. They had been married for 35 years with two grown sons, John Jr. and Peter. Both sons are married with children. John Jr. is a Financial Advisor and Peter is a pharmacist. Both live in the Nashville area so the Judge and Betsy could see their grandkids quite often. The Judge likes to golf, and Betsy is an avid tennis player. They support several local charities which kept Betsy quite busy. Judge Moran did not have to work. He was what you might call a Trust Fund Baby. But he had never been lazy even as a kid. His father demanded that he studied and worked hard and that was why he went to Law School at Vanderbilt. His father could afford to pay the tuition, but it wasn't easy getting through. Nevertheless, John worked hard, he got his law degree and he worked at his father's firm for a short time. He made the money; he loved law but he didn't like working at the injury firm whose goal was profit making. Probably because he had so much money all his life, he was never driven by getting more.

John rather gravitated towards public service. He wanted to do something larger than just himself. He left his father's firm much to his father's dismay and got a job as an Assistant District Attorney in the Nashville D.A.'s office. He loved the prosecution work. He stayed there for five years prosecuting all manner of criminal cases and he just fell in love with the courts and the criminal process in Nashville. John's colleagues at the D.A.'s office encouraged him to run for Judge when there was an opening on the Criminal Court that would hear all the felony cases. John had been in court so much, he respected the Judges and thought, *well, why not?* He started out at his dad's law firm, then the District Attorney's Office.

This would be something new for him. John had plenty of money for billboards and TV adds to run a strong campaign, and he did. He got elected to the Criminal Court and he had now been on the bench for 27 years. John loved it! He could walk away at any moment and never have to work another day in his life, but it was just not the person he was. He loved the bench, he loved being a Judge, he loved the law and all its intricacies. He loved the banter in the court room. He loved helping the little guy when he needed a break. He loved sentencing a really bad guy when he needed to be in prison to protect the community that he loved. John was 62 and a head full of gray hair. A little pudgy around the middle and he had a wry smile. He thought fast and talked slow. He had a southern drawl as slow as a child support check. All the lawyers admired Judge Moran because he always treated them and their clients with respect. He never lost his temper on the bench. He never yelled at the attorneys. He never belittled anyone. He never conducted anything other than a fair and constitutional court.

When you come before Judge Moran, you better be prepared. You better know the law, you better know the facts, you better know your evidence, you better have prepared your briefs and you better be on time. He didn't suffer shenanigans and he was more than willing to work overtime or even on Saturdays to get cases moved through his docket. Judge Moran was a true patriot, he loved America so much that he believed he had to stay on the bench because what he was doing was so important to help America function.

Monday Morning, Judge Moran got in his car and headed downtown to the courthouse. He had a light day today. He had arranged it that way. He had a trial for the past week for two people charged with murder during an armed robbery. The defense lawyers were battling it out with the D.A.'s prosecutors. The Judge was holding everyone's feet to the fire. Testimony was scheduled to resume at 1:00 pm today. He wanted to give the attorneys some time to come in this morning after that full week and to meet with their clients. Also, the Assistant District Attorney's would have time to strategize with their detectives. Then with all parties fully prepared, they could start the week just after lunch today. It was about 8:20 a.m. when the Judge got in his car and he headed down West End Avenue toward the Metro Courthouse. It usually took him about 40 minutes if there was some traffic and during this time of day there usually was. The Judge had a secure parking spot underneath the courthouse. But every morning he stopped at his favorite coffee shop on the corner of 3rd and Gay Street, one block north of the courthouse. It was the Moon-Shot Coffee Bar attached to the Town Place Hotel. The Judge habitually pulled into the paid parking lot across from the Moon-Shot and walked in to get his coffee. He paid monthly for the parking spot in advance. He liked to get his coffee, chat with people and walk in the sunshine to the front door of the Courthouse. He only used the underground parking during inclement weather. When the Judge pulled into the parking lot by the coffee shop, he parked in his usual reserved spot.

The Judge stepped out of his car and was instantly caught in a violent explosion that blew him back through his own vehicle, through the driver's side, as if someone had sent a cannon ball to his waist. Just for an instant, nails and ball bearings outnumbered musical notes in the atmosphere of the Music City. He was flexed in half and was sent sailing through the Buick he had driven downtown. He was mashed up against the passenger door which was also blown open. The Judge lay resting, mangled, just outside and on top of the passenger door of his own vehicle. He suffered massive wounds with his body being torn in half. Parts of the Judge were thrown all over the parking lot. His car was totally destroyed, and the dashboard was partially on fire. Smoke was rising from his vehicle. Car alarms had been set off throughout the parking lot as a result of the shock wave from the blast. People were screaming, others were running and there was an eerie quiet before someone could call 911 and the first sirens would begin to wail.

But this is downtown and Metro Police were everywhere. Within about 90 seconds the sirens began. First, it was radio cars, then fire engines, hook and ladder trucks, and ambulances. Officers running out of the courthouse and the secure booking across the street. Police officers being dispatched from Metro Police Headquarters on Murfreesboro Road. Motorcycle cops who had just arrived on duty that morning were swarming from all the downtown tributaries to help with the chaos. At this point, no one really knew what happened but everybody downtown who was outside or in buildings close by, heard the explosion. The blast was enormous.

Police radios were crackling, Police computer dispatch was asking for more cars from the central precinct. Lieutenant Mack of the Metropolitan Bomb Squad was called by the 911 dispatcher.

911 Dispatch introduced, "Lieutenant, this is the duty officer 911 dispatch."

Mack asked, "Yeah, what have you got?"

Dispatch replied, "We got a large explosion at 3rd and Gay streets right across from Central booking. We are going to need you right away."

Mack responded, "We are on our way."

Dispatch said, "10-4, thanks."

Lieutenant Mack hung up the phone. Explosion in the heart of downtown, one block from the Metro Courthouse, *it's going to be a long day* he thought. He yelled through the room to his sergeant.

Mack instructed, "Round up a squad, explosion at the 3rd and Gay near central booking. Get the bomb truck on the way. I'll call ATF."

Phone rings, woman answers. "ATF Nashville, how can I help you?"

Lieutenant Mack: "This is Lieutenant Mack Metro Police Bomb Squad. Is Bill Hightower in?"

The woman said, "Hold on please."

Bill Hightower introduced, "Hello, this is Bill Hightower."

Mack replied, "Bill, Lieutenant Mack."

Bill said, "Yeah, Mack."

Mack informed, "We just had a large explosion. 3rd and Gay Streets across from Central booking. I got the squad on the way, but we are going to need you guys too."

Bill responded, "Got it Mack, we are on the way."

Mack said, "Thanks."

Chapter Five:
Indefatigable Spirit

The police radio crackled loudly, "Any car in the vicinity of the Hideaway Bar, 21st and Lock? Any car in the vicinity of the Hideaway Bar, 21st and Lock? They are shooting up the place. Man with a gun, any car in the vicinity?"

"Forty-Seven to central Fifty-Two and Forty-Seven are a block away. We'll take the call." "OK, Forty-Seven. They're shooting it up right now. We're getting multiple calls. We'll send more cars." "10-4 Central."

Donnelly threw the radio mic back in the front seat of the Dodge, he looked up on the porch where his partner Jay was standing and yelled, "Jay, let's go, they are shooting up the Hideaway Bar!" Jay had been talking to a citizen on the porch taking a report of a break-in of an automobile when the call had come in. Donnelly and his partner were only a block away from the tavern on the same street. They could look down the street and see the neon sign for the Hideaway Bar. It was a drab; low rent place and Donnelly and all the other Deputies had been in it a number of times. On this beat, just north of Dade City, Florida the Pasco County Deputies were always busy. There were good people here but a lot of it was a hard scrabble life. In the shadows of the largest citrus packing plant in Florida, factory workers had small homes where they lived in an idyllic tropical climate but a good distance from the Gulf of Mexico. This was interior Florida, rural cattle ranches, citrus groves, miles and miles of orange trees where manual laborers picked the fruit for a multimillion-dollar citrus industry. The migrant labor was very poor. They would come from all over South America but mostly Mexico and would be housed in very squalid conditions in shacks that were often part of the orange grower's property. Migrant laborers were hard working people. They usually send money to their families back in Mexico, and save every dollar they could while trying to make a living by working in the hot sun. It wasn't an easy life. Yet, they were exploited, there was crime, there was violence and the deputies had to deal with all of it. One of the places where locals and migrants frequented was the Hideaway Bar. Donnelly and the other deputies knew it well. On a weekend night, you're almost certain to be there for a fight or a stabbing. Sometimes there are reports of shots fired. You could always go in there and catch someone with a gun or a knife, somebody wanted on a warrant. It was just a tough place. The Hideaway Bar was the kind of place where people that are emotionally deprived and living on the edge usually frequented. They go there to escape the storms and the stresses of life. *The irony*, Donnelly thought, *was that this place just magnifies those storms and turns their lives into a virtual hurricane of stress*. The place had the ambiance of a dumpster. If you tried to carve your initials into the bar, you'd have to carve them on top of someone else's. It wasn't exactly Peacock Alley, the bar at the famous Waldorf Astoria Hotel in New York City. No, ordering a Martini here would have the bartender looking at you like you had a snake on your head. Cheap beer, cheap whiskey, cheap thrills were the specialties offered here, while refinement was for some other place.

A couple of pool tables were in the back, with a roughhewn interior worn down to the bone. The patrons had haggard sun burned faces with skin that looked like it had been honed from years in the wind. *Mount Rushmore faces*, thought Donnelly. Time and sun had weathered and molded them. Some had a smile and some had a menacing grin, and the deputies had to decide the intent behind each face. Donnelly had gotten used to going into the place. Sometimes the trouble was in the back and you had to walk along the bar while all the patrons were on the bar stools. He had learned to pull his duty pistol out of his uniform holster and stick it into his gun belt right in front of his belly button when he would walk the length of the bar. Because, inevitably someone would try and grab your pistol even though it was snapped in the holster. Then you'd get distracted from the initial call, trying to arrest someone else. Sticking the gun down in your gun belt down low made sure nobody could grab it. It was just that kind of place.

But now, here was Donnelly and Jay just down the street with a report of the bar being shot up. As Jay raced down the steps from the porch and got to the cruiser, they both looked down the street towards the tavern and they could hear the shots. It was a Sunday evening and it was otherwise quiet. As they pulled open the cruiser doors, they saw a pick-up truck come fish-tailing out of the bar parking lot. The pick-up gunned its engine, and raced straight towards the deputy's car. A couple of seconds later, the driver's arm came out the side window and it was holding a handgun. Donnelly and Jay squatted down beside their cruiser, drew their duty weapons and as the pick-up truck flew by, the driver was firing shots out of the window at the two deputies. As they ducked down, the truck whizzed by, Donnelly's partner, Jay, managed to get off two rounds at the driver as it sped past.

Donnelly and Jay jumped in their cruiser and spun around, chasing the careening pick-up truck up 21st street towards Dade City. The driver was swerving all over the road, the radio cars were coming and screaming from every direction. The driver would stick his hand out the window waving his gun and occasionally firing a shot but he was clearly inebriated as the truck was speeding down the road crossing the center line and back time and time again. When he got onto the main road, he drove for about a half a mile and turned left into one of the neighborhoods. Rows of small Florida houses with leafy magnolia trees and palm trees dotted the lawns. The driver had slowed down now and took various turns down different residential streets with a string of sheriff's cars behind him. The Dade City police had now joined the chase as did the Florida Highway Patrol. Sirens were wailing, and radios were blaring as the deputies tried to get the mad man to stop. In just a few minutes, the truck careened off the side of the road, knocked down a stop sign and slammed into a tree. The truck wasn't going very fast when it hit the tree and the deputies all pulled up in their cruisers right behind it, jumping out with their shotguns and pistols ready to take on the shooter. The door to the truck opened and a white male in his 50's stepped out. He was rough looking. A working man, a farmer. *Someone who worked with his hands,* thought Donnelly. His right hand was in his trouser pocket and his left hand held a chihuahua. He swayed as he stood there looking at the spotlights of the deputy's cars. Squinting at the sea of red and blue flashing lights that confronted him. It was evening time and he was a strange pathetic figure bathed in the natural crepuscular light and the police light show. "Drop the God Damned Chihuahua.

 Hands in the air!" Donnelly yelled. The shooter just responded with expletives. "Get the fuck out of here. I ain't bothering nobody," he said.

"Drop that God Damned Chihuahua and put your hands where we can see them!" Donnelly yelled. Again, the shooter yelled back, "Get out of here, don't be bothering me! I ain't fucking with nobody!"

By now he had stepped a few feet away from the truck almost standing in the street and he was clearly drunk.

Donnelly thought they could get around the back of the truck and take him down without blowing his brains out with a shotgun. They figured he had the gun in his pocket but he was just so drunk it seemed like the best maneuver. Donnelly put the shotgun on the front seat of the cruiser and he and Jay snuck around the back of the shooters truck. While he was occupied looking at the other deputies and the flashing lights in his eyes, Jay and Donnelly tackled him on the street as the chihuahua ran whimpering off into the night. They quickly handcuffed him and pulled the revolver out of his pocket. They roughly dragged him over and threw him face down into the backseat of the radio car. As the deputies now congregated around the car, with the shooter in custody, they heard sirens in the distance from fire trucks and ambulances that had been called for the emergency.

Just then the police radio crackled again. "Any car at the Hideaway Bar? Any car at the Hideaway Bar?" Donnelly looked at Jay and he looked around at all the other deputies from the shift and he said, "Damn, I guess none of us ever made it to the Hideaway Bar." The dispatcher kept saying. "Any car at the Hideaway Bar? Any car at the Hideaway Bar?" Donnelly told Jay, "Let's go Jay, we need to get back up there." They jumped in their cruiser, pulled the radio out and said, "Forty-Seven, we're responding, we'll be there in a minute. One in custody, sixty-one will transport the prisoner, on our way to the Hideaway Bar." As they raced up to the Hideaway Bar, they could see a man laying down in the front parking lot with two other people with him. As the deputies pulled up and popped out like their asses were on fire, one of the citizens yelled, "He's been shot!" Donnelly could see the man was now sitting up. Apparently, they were tending to his leg. Donnelly said, "OK, the ambulance and the paramedics are on their way. They'll be here shortly." As Donnelly and Jay walked into the bar, they drew their duty weapons. No other radio car had made it to the bar since they were all chasing the known shooter down the street. *But was there another shooter?* wondered Donnelly. As they walked into the bar, the place where patrons would routinely fight with them and spit on them and try to grab their pistols on all their other calls, now seemed to be a very police friendly atmosphere.

As they walked in, they heard a voice say, "Thank God it's the cops!" Once Donnelly heard that, he could see numerous faces pop up from behind the bar as if they were prairie dogs, all coming out of their holes at the same time. Inching up just enough so you could barely see their eyes over the bar. Maybe a dozen or more of people. Donnelly said, "Is everybody alright back there?" "Yes! Yes!" was the reply. Donnelly could see numerous people laying on the floor who were shot. He stepped over two and there was another one by the pool table. There was a lot of moaning going on from the wounded. Donnelly walked to the back and he saw people hiding behind the pool table. As they finally stood up, they hollered,

"The cops! Thank God, the cops!" As he went and opened the bathroom door, there were about fifteen people jammed in that bathroom. Donnelly said, "It's alright, it's safe now, you can come out." As they came out of the bathroom, Donnelly uttered to himself, *just like a clown car.* He didn't think you could even fit that many people in that little bathroom. Just then paramedics and firefighters started streaming into the bar as Jay and other deputies out front directed them in. It was safe now and they just needed to attend to the wounded to see who was injured and to see if anybody had been killed. Donnelly went back outside, he could see the sergeant, the Shift Lieutenant and plain clothes detectives arriving. The sergeant saw Jay and Donnelly and said, "Good work guys. The next shift is already coming on so you guys need to go to the station and write your reports about all the gun play you were involved in. The captain is going to want to hear all the details so get it down on paper as quickly as you can so you don't lose anything." "OK Sarge, thanks," Donnelly said. Donnelly and Jay cruised back to the sheriff's station, talking about the events they had just experienced. They talked about how they handled it and if they could have done anything differently. How they were glad the shooter wasn't a very good shot. It seemed he had gotten angry at the bartender because he wouldn't serve him. He was so intoxicated that he was refused any more drinks. The witnesses said he was holding a chihuahua when he pulled a revolver out of his pocket and just started shooting into the crowd. He shot five people in the bar and another one outside as he was walking to his pick-up truck. He then got in his truck, reloaded and fired some shots as he was pulling out and fired at deputies seconds later. Jay shot from his duty weapon and just barely missed the shooter's head and put a hole in the steel of the pick-up truck, just above the back windshield. That could have ended it all right there. He would have never been able to hurt anybody after that.

Nevertheless, they had apprehended him to end the chaos. Donnelly wrote his report, got in his cruiser and went back home. He thought about his job and his chosen profession; his college degree in criminology and his police work. He liked being a uniform deputy. He liked the excitement of all of it and today sure was exciting. You could have been hurt or even killed his friends would tell him. They didn't want jobs like Donnelly had. None of his friends from college were policemen. They all had different professions. But he liked his. He thought it was interesting and exciting. He wasn't motivated much by money. He just wanted an interesting life and this sure gave it to him.

Donnelly liked being a cop, he liked everything about it. He liked the people he interacted with, he even liked the boring calls, reports of thefts, car break-ins, house break-ins, armed robberies, domestic assaults, car accidents, etc. He just relished all the activities. Sure, there were many boring times as well. Police work is kind of like that. Most of the work is routine stuff. Interacting with the public on their worst days. People who are down on their luck or have decided that crime is an easier way to make money than actually working. The days that are filled with excitement, like the shoot outs and the car chases are not an everyday occurrence. But every day was interesting to Donnelly. He liked the whole atmosphere of the job. He liked the paramilitary nature of it. He liked the uniform, the police cars, the symbolism, the badges, the guns, and the equipment. All of it was to be part and parcel of his persona. However, he was a man who liked the gentle touch. He could be as soft as a lover's caress or as hard as a New York pothole. But he preferred to go easy from the beginning. "Easy does it." He always said when trying to get people to comply with just a verbal command. One step at a time. Scale it up, go slow. Convincing them to go with you sure makes life easier. He learned that along the way when drunks would rip his uniform shirt, spit on him, bleed on him, and even kick him. He knew it just made a big mess of things and it wasn't going to result in any kind of serious prison time for a drunk in a bar fight. It wasn't easy to reason with a drunk and policemen learned that very quickly.

As much as he could on a weekend off, Donnelly would cruise down to his sister's house in Clearwater Beach, which was about an hour drive away. He would visit with her and his nephews and just have a relaxing day in the sun and water.

Donnelly loved the beach and he loved to go there to forget all about police work and his daily activities. Sure, he loved his job but he did need to escape it every once in a while. The weight of the problems of the citizens could not be taken on entirely by a deputy. A lot of that had to be left behind. Donnelly knew he couldn't save the world, he was just one small part of it, but he always wanted to do the right thing. A weekend at his sister's house would rejuvenate him so that he could get back to the work he loved in Pasco County. In the heart of some of the hard scrabble areas he patrolled, violence was endemic. He had seen his share of shootings, beatings, stabbing, murders and made a good number of arrests in cases like that. He had arrested husbands for beating their wives, caught and arrested vandals, fugitives, armed robbers, killers and burglars in the act. It was all routine police business that Donnelly enjoyed. He was extraverted. He especially liked testifying in court as a witness, being cross examined by the Defense attorneys and always playing by the rules. Donnelly believed he had to catch them fair and square and that's what made the difference between the good and the bad guys. *Twist the rules and you are no worse than they are* he thought. If they get away with it, well that's just the way the justice system was. But he learned to work within the system. He wanted to work by the rules to make his searches for evidence so good and his testimony so tight, and his investigations so thorough that it was hard to get away. This mattered, even when

Donnelly was working on small theft cases. Donnelly liked writing his police reports. His affidavits for complaints and warrants. He didn't mind it at all. He always saw it as his chance to get the facts down, to play by the rules, and to win the conviction. To do a good job. He noticed that many of his fellow deputies hated writing reports and they tried to make them as short as possible. Not Donnelly, no, he wanted to be as thorough as possible. If he had to write a longer report, so be it. He wanted the facts laid out plain and simple so they could be tried in the court and the juries would decide. He got along famously with the states attorneys who were prosecutors on the cases because they liked his thorough work. They appreciated his direct and clear testimony and they took many of his cases on. Donnelly enjoyed working with the detectives on a case if he was the first uniform deputy on the scene of a crime. Robbery, murder, he would, no matter what, do a thorough job to the best of his abilities to help the detectives make the apprehension.

It was just such a case, one night when Donnelly was working a beat near Zephyrhills, Florida.

"Central to Forty-Seven."

"Forty-Seven, Go ahead Central."

"Armed robbery reported at the market, Highway 301 at the cross-street intersection. A silent alarm has been tripped in the market for a robbery."

"10-4 Central, in route."

Dispatch yelled, "Car Sixty-One;

Deputy yelled also, "Sixty-One."

Dispatch ordered, "Sixty-One, back up Forty-Seven for a robbery at the market on Highway 301 and Cross-street just north of Zephyrhills."

"10-4, Sixty-One responding."

Robbery calls were pretty routine for that part of Florida. *Every fugitive on earth wanted to go to Florida* Donnelly always thought. They commit a crime in every state and where do they go, Florida. Just like the tourists. Even the criminals want the sunshine and the beach. Here they come, they have no money, nowhere to live but they got a gun so they start knocking off markets on their way south. Unbelievable! Of course, they had their share of local robbers as well. But there were so many transient ones that it was sometimes hard to break the cases. It was just a constant thing at the small "stop and robs" as all the deputies called them. Sometimes they were violent. The armed robbers would shoot the clerk and kill or wound them, and sometimes they end up raping the clerk after filling their pockets with money from the cash drawer. Donnelly even had clerks raped right in the aisle. They would be in and out of the store in just a few minutes, so Donnelly sped to this call, his top lights flashing but no siren. There wasn't much traffic on the streets. He wanted to see if he could slip in there quick. He pulled up to the side of the market but he saw no activity. He saw all the store lights were on. There was only one car parked in front. He didn't see any people. He got out of his cruiser, got his duty weapon out and entered the market carefully, slowly, keeping cover. As he stepped in, he saw that the cash drawer was open but nobody in sight. Two more steps around the counter and there he saw the clerk laying in a pool of blood. The clerk had been shot in the head. Donnelly quickly went over and checked the clerk's pulse but they were clearly deceased. He then swept through the market, through the coolers and went to the back to make sure there was no one else inside. He got back on his radio and told dispatch to send homicide detectives as it looked like a murder scene. The back-up cars arrived, then the sergeants, the lieutenants, fire trucks, and paramedics. Neighbors across the street filled the area.

Donnelly went out to the front to his cruiser that was parked outside, took out his note pad, laid it on the hood of his car and started making his initial notes. He then started walking over to the crowd of neighbors that had gathered and asked if anybody had seen anything. Routine, neighborhood check: Interview the witnesses, get their names, write down what they said, what they saw, if anything, etc. This was important because the report will be used someday and what the witnesses had initially said could be important to the case. Donnelly located a witness who stated that they saw a Dodge Charger, black in color at the market just prior to the deputy's arrival and that it had sped off at a high rate of speed. The most notable thing, according to the witness was that the hood was missing on the car. The witness didn't get a look at the tag or the occupants but just said it was a loud car and it sped away and had no hood.

Donnelly notified dispatch of a description of a suspect vehicle in the homicide at the market. He also relayed that to the detectives on the scene. Donnelly was still interviewing witnesses in front of the market when forty-five minutes later a deputy working in a zone about thirty miles east of the store spotted a car matching the description. A black Dodge Charger with no hood. The deputy pulled the car over and arrested the two occupants. He found the murder weapon on them. *Cased closed* Donnelly thought. A good witness and a neighborhood check. Nice work by the patrol deputy who made the arrest. Team work all the way around. Maybe these guys won't be able to kill anyone else.

Chapter Six:
Molded by History

Donnelly wanted something more. He wanted his career to grow and he wanted to grow with it. He wanted more training; he wanted more interesting duties. He wanted to get into criminal investigation deeper. He was young and he wanted to try new things. He watched all the other agents from various other law enforcement agencies come and go while they were interacting with deputies and detectives in his department; State agents from the Florida Department of Law Enforcement, Federal agents from The Federal Bureau of Investigations (FBI), The Drug Enforcement Administration (DEA), The Bureau of Alcohol, Tobacco and Firearms and Explosives (ATF) and The United States Marshall's Service. (USMS) The United States Customs Service (USCS) and The Internal Revenue Service (IRS) and state troopers and detectives from the bigger cities. He'd seen them all come through. He talked to them; he was always interested in what they were doing. He tried to find out more about their work. The guys that interested Donnelly the most was the Special Agents of the ATF. They seemed to have the most interesting cases they were working, like someone in possession of machine guns that they were after or they were trying to trace down members of a biker gang for making a bomb. Either they were asking about a Ku Klux Klan member who was supposed to be making hand grenades, or they were after some convicted felon who had stolen guns. Everything they seemed to do was challenging and interesting and it surrounded violence and violent crime. Donnelly was drawn to that type of work and he found these Special Agents from the Tampa Office to be pretty cool guys. He made some inquiries and found out where he could take the exam to be an ATF Special Agent in the Federal Service.

Donnelly took the exam and later got a call for an interview. He went down to Tampa and in an office building downtown, he faced a panel of three ATF Commanders from around the country. They had interviewed him about all the requirements. They questioned him about his life and his police work. Getting a job with the ATF was very competitive and the waiting room for the interview was filled with detectives and officers from departments from across Florida all vying for a position as a Federal Agent. Donnelly thought to himself, *this competition is stiff, I'm not sure I'll have a chance here.* In a couple of weeks, he got a letter with a return address of ATF Headquarters, Washington DC. Donnelly thought, *it can only be one of two ways. This will let him know whether they say thanks a lot, or congratulations, you're hired.* When he opened the letter, he was excited to see that they were offering him a position with the ATF. He had to go through physical examinations, doctor's exams and of course go through their rigorous training at the ATF Academy at the Federal Law Enforcement Training Center. *More academies* thought Donnelly. He had already been through the police academy and now he'll have to go through another one to learn how to handle people and to shoot a gun again. But he'll just have to do it if he wants this job. He wasn't sure he was going to learn a whole lot of new things. Donnelly's life was about to enter a new phase.

Tim Donnelly was a funny guy, in a dead serious job. He was not funny in the weird or awkward way, rather he was witty and always spitting out a joke or a quip making everyone smile. It was as though laughter was his raison' d'tre, but it wasn't. That was his work, his career was his passion. The humor was just intrinsic to him, and he needed it like we all need oxygen. Donnelly successfully completed the ATF Academy and was a Special Agent. His father was a Clearwater detective Lieutenant and Tim followed in his footsteps, while his mother was an ER Nurse. His parents met in the ER when his dad was a patrolman. He had two younger sisters; one is a pediatrician, while his other sister died in a boating accident when she was 18. That accident drove Tim and his other sister to become very close. She is married with three beautiful boys. They love their Uncle Tim and he loves them too. When he was on the sheriff's department, he spent a lot of his off time at his sister's hanging out and playing with her kids. He would play ball and take them to the beach in his convertible. He would go to any baseball game they had. They loved hanging out with him because was fun and funny.

Now that he is in Nashville, he doesn't get to see them that often. But he frequently stays in touch. After having ascended the ranks, he was the Special Agent in Charge of the top field Command position in the federal law enforcement service. He worked for the Bureau of Alcohol, Tobacco Firearms and Explosives, ATF. The "E" was officially silent and not used in the acronym of the agency and Donnelly always made a joke of that. Just like ATF Headquarters he would say, silent, especially anytime he needed more resources. ATF was an agency that had a unique American History. Donnelly was proud to work for ATF. It was a strong and important agency with a long legacy, and all the police and other law enforcement professionals knew it well.

Although not well-known to the public as its sister agencies, the FBI or the Secret Service, the ATF was involved with the nation's most violent crimes and significant cases involving guns, bombs, and arson.

Donnelly liked to say that the first ATF agent was George Washington, who took 10,000 militia men to Pennsylvania in 1794 to put down the whiskey rebellion. Washington knew that unless the law was enforced on the whiskey tax that there would be no nation. The government needs a treasury department to produce revenue. That revenue comes from taxes and tariffs off the backs of the citizens. For almost 200 years, the federal agents who enforced the laws on the whiskey tax were assigned to the Treasury Department. The Treasury was a major law enforcement department of the United States Government. In the past, it had housed the ATF, United States Secret Service, the United States Custom Service, and the Coast Guard. In addition, it housed the Internal Revenue Service. Donnelly had been to Washington and had served there on a permanent basis and had been to the Treasury Department many times. Treasury was the building located immediately adjacent to the White House. Arguably the most important department when our nation was formed.

When bootleggers and whiskey makers killed treasury agents in Pennsylvania who were assigned to enforce the whiskey tax, President Washington knew he had to make a stand. The tax on whiskey was needed to pay for the revolutionary war debt. He put down the rebellion with his militia men and brought law and order and control back to the United States government in Washington. In the nascent United States, there was no internal income tax. The nation ran on a tax on whiskey and tobacco from the Virginia colonies and the tariffs enforced by the revenue cutter service which later became the US Lifesaving Service and the United States Coast Guard. Years later, in the midst of the civil war, Confederate states were printing counterfeit union money to inflate the economy of the north. President Abraham Lincoln appointed three detectives assigned to the Treasury

Department to root out the counterfeit bills. Those agents were designated to operate in secret and to work undercover to find and arrest the counterfeiters. So, their name was coined as the Secret Service, Agents of the United States Treasury Department.

When President Lincoln was assassinated at Ford's Theatre, right at the end of the civil war, his only protection in the theatre with him was a military adjutant who was an Army Lieutenant. President William McKinley was assassinated in 1901 and the duties of protecting the Executive after two assassinations fell to the Treasury Agents of the Secret Service. At this time in America's history there was no FBI, there was no Homeland Security. There were just the agents of the Treasury department, U.S. Marshall's and Postal Inspectors. In the twenties when Congress passed the Volstead Act which prohibited the distillation and sale of liquor, more US Treasury Agents were needed to enforce prohibition. And so, a full bureau was formed inside the Treasury Department named 'The Bureau of Prohibition'. Treasury agents were assigned to bust up illegal distilleries and bootlegging operations. And became famous chasing the gangsters in the 20's and 30's during those gangland days.

Donnelly liked to get up in front of the new class of special agents or new police officers out of the academy and ask them who they thought the most famous FBI agent was. Inevitably, the recruits would shout out names like, J Edgar Hoover, Melvin Purvis,

Elliott Ness, etc. Donnelly would pause, Elliott Ness, that's the name he was looking for. But Ness was never an FBI agent, he was an agent assigned to the Treasury Department's Bureau of Prohibition, the forerunner of the ATF. That bureau was also under the Justice Department at some point but nevertheless, when prohibition was repealed, the name had to be changed to the Alcohol Tax Unit, the slang was "revenuers" because they protected the revenue of the United States.

With the repeal of prohibition, violence didn't come to an end. Gangsters were still involved in crime, bootlegging, murder and extortion which still had to be controlled by law enforcement and agents of the Federal Government. That era saw many violent gangland shootings where gangsters of the 20's and 30's would drive by on a city street and blast tommy guns at rival gangsters. The Saint Valentine's Day massacre in Chicago where rival gangsters from Al Capone's gang, disguised as policemen and murdered members of the Northside Bugs Moran gang. The gangsters that were in the headlines were names like Dillinger, Machine Gun Kelly, and Alvin "Creepy" Karpis and Machine Gun Jack McGurn. Congress had to respond to the violence and they passed a law called the "National Firearms Act." This act regulated the sale of machine guns, silencers, hand grenades, sawed-off shotguns, pen guns, cane guns and what the Congress titled "gangster type weapons".

Who was given the responsibility to enforce these laws? The same federal agents who were chasing the gangsters all along and who had the authority under the law, the agents under the Treasury Department, now known the Alcohol Tax Unit. Elliott Ness famously led a group of Chicago agents in the Bureau of Prohibition who were incorruptible. A Chicago reporter, reportedly gave them the name the "Untouchables" because they were the only group of police and agents who could not be paid off or scared away to enforce the law and to do their duties without fear or favor. The agency later picked up the Tobacco tax enforcement responsibilities and that name was added to their title by Congress. Since congress included firearms enforcement responsibilities, they then added (firearms) to the agency's name and it became known as Alcohol, Tobacco, Firearms which we now know as the ATF. Since 1934, the ATF had many responsibilities in the explosives area since bombs and hand grenades were regulated under the 1934 National Firearms Act. These agents worked on such cases and that responsibility was enhanced in 1970 by the Federal Explosives Control Act, which again gave the ATF many new responsibilities in the explosives arena. The name explosives was later added to the official name of the agency but the acronym remained the ATF.

Donnelly knew that the agency had asked Congress to change the name to make it something simpler so that the public could understand it because it was very confusing. Strong lobby groups from the firearms industry and the alcohol industry never wanted the name to be changed for various reasons that were politically motivated, so they lobbied Congress not to change the name. But Donnelly knew it didn't matter. The work that was done by the special agents of the ATF was known to the law enforcement community, was known to the citizens they worked with, and was known to the courts and the Judges. The people who were knowledgeable about what really happened in law enforcement and on the streets of America.

Now, Donnelly was the Special Agent in Charge of the Nashville division of the ATF which encompassed the states of Tennessee and Alabama. He had offices from Mobile on the gulf coast all the way to Knoxville and the mountains of East Tennessee, and as far west as the Mississippi. He had cities like Birmingham, Nashville, and Memphis with multiple squads and lots of violent crime to work on. He had mountain men and militia men in East Tennessee and North Alabama. He had Nazis and Klansmen. He had bombers and killers. Clandestine silencer factories. People making automatic parts for pistols and rifles that turned them into machine guns. He had street crime to deal with in most of these big cities, gangs like MS13 or Crips, and Bloods were also major targets of ATF. And while all this work was going on, they were always being beat up politically by elements of the gun lobby who like to use the agency as a whipping boy in the Congress. Whether Congress was trying to pass a law in the firearms arena or not, there was always a chance for weak kneed Congressmen with no backbone to beat up on an agency. There was little risk to themselves. Agencies generally couldn't fight back, as they had to fight with both hands tied behind their back and they just had to take the punches from any unhinged Congressmen who clearly had a few tiles loose. This affected budgets and morale. Donnelly knew there was only one way to get through it. He always remembered Winston Churchill's quote. "If you're going through Hell, keep going." And that is what Donnelly always did when the political winds were battering the ATF in the news or in the Congress.

Donnelly was in his early 40's just starting to get a little gray hair, but he had been a cop since he was 21, and at the age of 26 he went to the ATF. He had always carried a gun, he had always been in law enforcement, his college degree was criminology and he loved his career. It was his passion in life. He was a member of the United States Government Senior Executive Service which is highest paid and highest-ranking civilian position in the government and the Special Agent in Charge was the highest-ranking civilian position in the Federal Service in the field. Donnelly loved the field; he had done two tours of ATF headquarters in Washington DC and he did not like the work at all. It was just too confining, too bureaucratic and just too boring. Donnelly craved the investigations; he craved the action. He wanted to be out there with the sheriff's, the chiefs, and the prosecutors. He wanted to talk to the victims of crimes and he liked the media presence. The job of Special Agent in Charge was akin to being a chief of police because you would have many squads under you, agents with badges and guns that made arrests, served warrants and who investigated crime. He had to deal with the press and the politicians, he had to deal with people who suffered from criminals, he had to deal with violence, investigations and he had to deal with, most of all, constant pressure. Donnelly like to say, "If you ever took the pressure off, you'd get the bends." This is because he was so used to dealing in a pressure cooker.

Donnelly had just broken up with his girlfriend, she was a beautiful girl and he was infatuated with her. Her name was Dawn Bennett. They had been together steady for almost four years. Donnelly met her when she was a flight attendant while he was flying out to Los Angeles for an assignment. She was tall, light hair, hazel eyes and a beautiful smile. Dawn and Donnelly loved trips to the beach, hanging out, going out around Nashville and just enjoying life but both of them had demanding careers that could pull them apart. A year after they met, Dawn had left the airline and started a modeling career. At first, she had to travel from Nashville to get her photo shoots and she was gaining more and more success in the modeling industry. Then the opportunity came for her with a modeling agency in New York City with tons of work and a higher pay but she had to relocate to the Big Apple. Although they tried to work it out but it just wouldn't be so. Donnelly would not leave his career; it was his passion and Dawn was getting the biggest break of her life. They tried the long-distance test a few months but it just was not going to happen, so they mutually decided to end the relationship. Both of them, professionals at their respective careers immersed themselves into their work. Donnelly became so focused on all the tasks and responsibilities of being the boss that he was not consumed with trying to find a new girl, Dawn had just happened when he wasn't looking. He thought to himself *the next one would as well.*

Donnelly was an extravert. He liked being around and meeting people. Whenever he was off duty, he would be out listening to music, go to various clubs, etc. He never drank hard liquor or wine; just Irish stouts. Donnelly had one rule; he never drove a car if he had even one beer. He would say he is the "King of Uber", everywhere he went it was always by Uber. He had a hard line in the sand. Either you are drinking or you are driving. Never at the same time and he never wavered on it. Nevertheless, Donnelly always had a large Uber bill because he was always around town seeing people and laughing, talking, making friends, men and women, groups of people, telling jokes, etc. He just drew energy from other people. As strange as it may seem, this did not lead Donnelly to join any organizations or clubs. He called himself a Nomad.

He didn't want to be a member of any club, to elect officers, to have votes, to have treasuries, presidents, vice presidents, rules, dues, and meetings. All of that was just work to him. He had enough of that at ATF; organizations, conference calls, meetings, etc. He hated administrative work; he didn't like budget meetings to see how many cars were needed to be purchased or how many radios, police equipment, furniture or new office space were needed. All of this detail bored him endlessly; he could not stand to be around it.

But the way Donnelly dealt with it was to make sure he had highly trained competent and trusted people around him who could take care of such matters, and then empower them to do the job without interfering or micromanaging their duties. Donnelly had a budget officer in Nashville, her name was Kathy. He gave her total power to run the budget of the Nashville Division and she was an expert at it. Donnelly told her, "I don't want to be involved in any budget meetings. I don't want to know anything about the budget. All I want you to do is to never overspend the money Washington gives us and always be responsible with the tax payers funds." Kathy was a real pro. A Management Analyst, as her position was called. She ran the budget for his division like no one else. In fact, when Donnelly was in Washington, the budget chiefs would always say, "Donnelly, your division runs the budget better than any other division in America. You never over spend; your reports are always on time and up to date. We never have to worry about anything from your division. You are doing a great job." Donnelly would just smile, and say "Thank you, it is really just my budget officer. She's the best." They would acknowledge that and ask if Kathy could come and train all the other budget officers for all the other divisions. Donnelly always thought to himself, *it wasn't magic, it came down to trusting the people who work for you and making sure they had the proper training, credentials and then leaving them the hell alone.*

Don't fret over everything that happens, don't get in their business, don't micromanage what they do. Just trust them to get the job done. They will do it better than anybody else. And that is the way Donnelly always ran his divisions, he trusted his people, he empowered his people, and he made his subordinate supervisors to empower their people. Push power down, push it down, and push it away. The more you push power down, the more powerful you get. That was a concept many people just could not understand, but Donnelly knew it instinctively.

Donnelly loved hotrod cars. On the weekends, he would take his old 66 out and drive it to some cruise-ins and car shows and talk to his buddies, tinker with his engine. He was pretty adept at it and he loved doing it. But now it was Monday morning and he was passionate about getting back to work.

But today would be one of those dead serious days. Donnelly had all his supervisors and his three

Assistant Special Agents in Charge around a conference table and more scattered across Tennessee and Alabama on the speaker phone. His Nashville field Division encompassed those two states, and it was always busy.

His division had about 1000 open cases across the two states and they were all intertwined with acts of violence throughout those communities. He had three principal deputies that ran another 16 subordinate supervisors that all ran squads of approximately 10 special agents or investigators. On Monday morning, Donnelly had a quick staff meeting. He had his assistant Special Agents in Charge and local supervisors in the conference room and the rest of the supervisors in the two states on a conference call.

He didn't like meetings at all. He wanted to get down and dirty. He wanted the facts; he wanted the hard stuff and he wanted to get things moving. He felt meetings were time wasters. He just did not like bureaucracy. So, with Donnelly, his meetings always moved very quickly and here they were around 9:00 a.m., at a command meeting on a Monday morning. With Donnelly, this meeting would be over in thirty minutes at the most. He would get the principal staff and give everyone their orders and they would move on to the week's operations.

About ten minutes into the meeting, one of the agents from the intelligence group knocked on the door and came into the meeting and whispered into the ear of the Agent in Charge of the Intelligence group. That supervisor said, "Thanks," and the intelligence agent left. The supervisor then told Donnelly and everyone in the meeting and on the call that we just received a report of a bombing in downtown Nashville one block north of the Metropolitan Courthouse and there are reports of fatalities. Donnelly knew what that meant; it was going to be a long week. He ordered his supervisors, "Let's get moving guys. Let's get that bomb truck down there and get all of our explosive specialists down there and let's get the National Response Team leader on the phone and tell him we will give him an assessment in a couple of hours. And I'll head down there myself."

Chapter Seven:
Evil Comes Calling

Murder is a simple thing, the killer thought. Everybody mistakenly thinks it is really difficult, but it's not. A life can be taken in many ways. A human being is really a fragile thing. What's harder is getting away with it. Getting away with it so that you can enjoy it, and enjoy the fruits of your actions. Humanity is a septic tank. He learned that over his many years. It just takes for one to have the guts and the smartness to crawl out of the top, push off the lid and get out into the sunshine. Everyone else wants to wallow down in the putrid muck, but this killer doesn't. He wants to go out on top and look down on the losers below, that is how he always desires and plans it.

He's not like those crazed mass shooters whose only real goal was suicide after choking on some empty grudge. They strap bandoleros across their chest, like some stereotypical Mexican bandit from a cheesy old bigoted Hollywood movie. They rush into their work place or some public establishment to slaughter the innocent, as if that's an act worth remembering. To him, they are worth no more than the rubber mat in the bottom of a man's public urinal, they deserve to be pissed on over and over again. Who would do such a thing, kill for no benefit? Killers like this are the ones who aren't even wanted in Hell. No, Hell has a place for those who kill for a purpose, a reason, or for something to gain, not just fanatics who went around with their hair on fire shooting buckets of bullets out of their newly acquired military style rifle. Their ill-fitting bullet-proof vests and tactical gear makes them look like a simpleton in a carnival side show. They dispense a lot of heartache for sure. A lot of crying and weeping and moaning. He didn't care about any of that. He wasn't even sympathetic to the survivors. No, they are just part of the septic tank as he sees them. He had no sympathy for any of them. But he had admiration on for those who killed for a reason, for a purpose just like he did, to gain something, to get the edge, and to move to sit next to the throne in Hell. The devil's right-hand man. That chair was reserved for those like him, who are bad enough to act with purpose, thought, and intelligence. That's who the Devil admired and that's what he was going to be.

He had killed before; those were with a purpose as well and spaced far apart. He wasn't some serial killer seeking notoriety or fame through his murders. That didn't interest him at all. He wanted no infamy for what he did. He did not even want to be known for what he did. In fact, he wanted no one to know. *It was between him and Beelzebub* he thought. He had no real friends. He had one person he admired in his whole life. The rest of the world could go to hell, to eternal damnation, to the very bottom of the pit where they could serve at his feet. The job this week had been a long time coming. He had no employer that wanted him to do something like this. No, this was for him, but it was a task nonetheless; a mission, a calling really. Something he had to do. He always wanted to work to make things right. Right for him, right in his world, not right for the world. He wouldn't kill someone just because they were famous, or good or bad. He could care less. No, he had to have a reason that affected him directly, that was good for him specifically. A mission that would help him, one that would let him gain something. That was paramount. Your own desires, your own self-interest, that's what mattered.

So, this murder, which would occur in a few days, had been on his mind for a long time. He'd scoped it out and he'd staked it out. He knew just how to do it, but more importantly, just how to get away with it. Getting away with it was half the battle. In addition, you would gain an immense satisfaction from delivering pain to someone that you hated more than you could even describe. You could also gain the added benefit of being able to pin it on another person that you detested intensely as well. It was kind of similar to buy one get one free on the center aisle at Walmart. Above all else, he craved the satisfaction of revenge and benefits of the plan he was about to accomplish this week. *Kill one, frame one, what could be better?* He chuckled as he thought about his plan. The plan and all if its machinations were going to make him very, very happy.

Preparations are key, cops nowadays have gotten too dang smart. They had fancy laboratories, DNA analysis, hair, blood and fingerprint analysis, not to mention the fact that cameras were everywhere. It wasn't easy like it used to be. Things were different now, much more difficult. And getting away with something took more planning and effort. But that is what excited him the most. The killing was the easy part. The revenge, the sweet part, but getting away with it was the singularly spectacular part. That was the crème de' la crème. The first step in accepting his throne and scepter. You have to show that you are smarter than all those cops, than all those people who thought they could get you. Yes, that was a giant reward in and of itself. You didn't want them to ever know who you were. Infamy was overrated. You didn't want it; you get your slice of it later. He relished the thought of laying on the searing hot bed springs of Hell, enjoying the pain and thinking about all the people that he had destroyed, upended and demolished, that was pure victory.

So, the mechanics of this killing were critical. Two people lived in the house but he was only after one. He wanted the woman.

She was going to die a slow and agonizing death. He had to make sure the husband was gone. He didn't want any interference, he didn't want it to be messy, he didn't want to kill both of them. No, he just wanted the woman. But he needed the husband to be far away. Far away so he could have time to take his time. So, he carefully planned and watched. He carefully learned the schedule to perfection. He knew when the man in the house would be gone on his trip this weekend. So, he prepared his tools, his clothes and his methods. Unlike amateur TV killers, who dress all in black head to toe. He wouldn't have any of that buffoonery, as he was not a graduate of clown college. *That corny all black dress just made you a target,* he mused. If someone saw you on the sidewalk or in an alley dressed like that, they would immediately call 911. That's all for greenhorns and crime TV. No, that's not how he would operate, he was too smart for that.

The first thing was how he was going to approach the residence because it was critical in these days with all the private security cameras. Ring doorbells, cameras on every store and gas station. Security cameras were ubiquitous. He would probably be seen by some, so he had to account for that. It is what they saw that mattered after all. As long as you weren't identifiable, traceable, a figure going by didn't matter. What you didn't want them to see was your tag number or your face or clothing they could trace. That was all very critical. With that in mind he had scouted the neighborhood many, many, times. He'd driven and walked the streets. In fact, his car had been seen through there at various times over the past year. He actually walked the sidewalks on most occasions. Maybe a passerby might have seen him at one time, yet he was a very plain looking fellow. He never stared anybody in the eye. He always looked like he had a reason to be there. The area was pretty densely populated with apartments and homes so just another man walking on the street with his dog, wouldn't arouse anything suspicious. In fact, the killer's dog was key. He had a small border collie, black and white, not very big, but this dog was special. He took it to a veterinarian in Louisiana a year ago when he started the plan for this killing and paid the veterinarian to do a clandestine operation. He wanted the dog's vocal cords cut. He told the vet that his wife is very sick and could not sleep at night with the dog barking at every shadow, but she couldn't bear to part with him. Of course, it was all a lie, he had no wife. The dog was just a tool, a tool for his upcoming murder, he had no reason to have an iota of care for the dog other than as a means to his goals. The veterinarian did as instructed and at the cost of $5,000.00, but he was happy with the result. The dog couldn't bark, couldn't even whimper, he was a silent dog and that was just what the killer wanted. He'd nursed him back to health; he fed him regularly. *You don't want to abuse your tools* he thought. You want to keep them oiled and stored in a dry place. You want them to work when they are needed. The same with the dog. After the killing was over, he'd get rid of the dog. Just a minor step in his post event planning.

He did not live in the same town where he was going to commit this murder so he had to do some travelling. He had to cover his tracks on that too. He didn't want to stay in any motels, or places where he had to register or where they could see his car. He had to plan that very carefully. He found a place where he could park quite a distance from the target house. He had to walk quite a long way. It was a place near a park where his car wouldn't be noticed. There seemed to be no cameras around. He could get out with the dog and walk a mile and a half on the sidewalk and get to the target event without being spotted. He'd have plenty of time to escape as well as no one would know he did it. Not right away anyway. His dress for the killing would be very simple; jogging shoes, blue jeans, just a navy color Dickie's work shirt, and a light cotton jacket that was tan. He was plain in countenance except for his dead black unforgettable eyes, medusa like, they could cause a person's spine to feel chilled as cold stone. He knew how his eyes affected people so he had a ball hat that he could pull down low. He always wore a very carefully applied but fake mustache when he walked in that area with the dog. He'd had a professional make-up artist do it for him in Atlanta. He told the artist that he was going to be in a special play in another town and he needed the mustache to look absolutely authentic. What a job that make-up artist had done. No one who ever saw it even thought twice about it because it looked so real. It cost money, of course, to get it done professionally. You can't just stick on something that everybody will recognize instantly as fake. Like some beclowned bank robber destined to be caught. No, it had to be different and be able to pass muster when you walk past someone on the street, even if they talk to you for just a minute it had to pass as real and this one surely did. In addition to the mustache, he discovered a way to make a fake blemish on his neck that really stood out. It was almost purple in color, a slash along the left side of his neck that ran about six inches. He would wear his shirt open so anyone he talked to couldn't help but notice it. It was somewhat of a cross between a scar and a birth mark, purplish in color but immediately noticeable. Not something any witness could ever forget. Of course, he only wore it when he was to be seen near the scene of the murder just in case a

witness reported seeing him. The plan was that nobody would see him and that he could get in and out without a witness anywhere nearby.

His plan was to park the car, take the border collie that he had named Whisper and walk to the target house. It was all a residential area and there was a great chance of Ring doorbells catching his figure as he went by. But he would have Whisper with him no matter what. He would have the outfit that he never wore anywhere near his home or anyplace else. He only wore it in that neighborhood only on that night and it was to be destroyed immediately after. He had his mustache and scar, his baseball hat pulled low. He would be walking by in the darkness. Yes, a doorbell camera might catch a figure walking a dog but that was about it. No one even knew he had the dog because it didn't bark, it was so quiet and he never took the dog out of his house. Not one of his own neighbors knew he had a dog because he usually left him in his basement in a box. If a neighbor was ever questioned if he had a dog, they would say, "No. He hates dogs and cats." Of course, it was true, he did. So, even if a ring doorbell would happen to catch an image of the killer with a dog, it would never put any suspicion on him. But he would be so far removed that it was unlikely that his name would ever surface in the matter. It just took very careful planning. He was smarter than all of the detectives. As

Shakespeare wrote, "Every why has a wherefore." And his wherefore was that his plan was as deep as Jeff Bezos's pockets. They are just stupid cops. Take off the uniform, they buy cheap suits. They get lucky once in a while but they were still inadequate in their job. He wasn't dumb, no he wasn't dumb.

The target house had one camera over the front porch. He had scoped it out many times. He knew exactly where it was and how he could get around through the back alley quietly. He would tie Whisper up to where he'd never be seen to make his way into the house. He would know that the man was gone when the pickup truck was no longer seen in the driveway. He knew that the woman he hated with a passion would be home alone and he would be free to let out his vengeance on her. Oh, he wanted to do it so slowly. She didn't deserve a fast death. He thought about it, he thought about it every night for years. How he would do it, how slowly he would do it, and how he would make her suffer for all the wrong she had done in her life. All the time he had would give him the incentive to go very slow and it was as if her pain would be releasing his joy. Each time she would experience the pain, he would get the compounded joy and thrill from watching her suffer. It was going to be such a magical night, wickedly amazing. He had everything he hoped for all planned out.

As he prepared his tools for that week, he was obsessed with getting it right. He was very aware of bloody shoe tracks leading straight to the killer. He made sure he had gotten some surgical booties to cover his shoes to help disguise his shoe size and tread, which he can discard when he's finished. He was checking the weather to make sure everything was favorable. He had to have his dress coincide with the weather so he didn't stick out. He scouted the neighborhood so well; he knew when the normal dog walkers were off the street, usually about a half hour past dark. That would be perfect timing for when the man left the house. He wanted it in the late evening. He had everything timed perfectly. The weather was going to cooperate. Everything was right. His vehicle, the one he rarely used and has never taken it to that neighborhood before was all gassed up and ready to go. It was very nondescript, gray in color, and hardly noticeable. A small four door sedan. *Unremarkable* is what he thought, as unremarkable as it can be. He wanted it plain in every way. He wanted no one to notice.

Friday night came and his plan began. He left his car at the far back corner of the park. He walked a mile and half; he tied up the dog and made a stealth entry into the home. No one would even be able to find anything there that would lead back to him. He confronted the bitch in the kitchen, and when she turned and saw him, she gasped. She had a dog that started barking non-stop. He was prepared. He had a whole pocket of dog treats and he threw them on the floor toward the living room. The dog happily started for the treats. He had on a rubber clown mask, black gloves and a K-bar knife in his right hand. He raised his left hand to his mouth, put his finger to his lips and said, "Shhh." It didn't work though, as the bitch started to scream. He stepped across the room and with his fist wrapped around the knife handle, punched her right in the face. Knocking her back against the counter and bloodying her nose. "You scream one more time and I'll jam this knife right through your heart you dirty bitch," he said in a practiced whisper, not in his normal voice.

Her eyes were wide with terror, the killer slapped her back and forth a couple of times with his left hand and spun her around as she was facing the kitchen counter. As she gripped the counter with all her might, he grabbed the back of her hair, put the K-bar knife to her throat and pulled her head back. With the clown mask still on, he says, now in his normal voice, "Shut up you bitch." Her eyes grew wide with anger. "IT'S YOU!" she said. "Yep, it's me," he answered. "You'll never get away with this you know. I will tell the cops everything," she said. "Shut the FUCK up!" he yelled. "You do exactly as I say bitch or I will cut your throat from ear to ear." He tried to pull her arms behind her but she wouldn't cooperate, they struggled for a few minutes with her facing the kitchen counter. Eventually, he overwhelmed her and finally got control of both of her hands.

He then pulled a zip tie from his pocket and tied her hands behind her back with it. She had been bleeding from her nose all over the kitchen counter and the floor, and he stepped in it as they walked out of the kitchen toward the basement. Of course, he knew the exact layout of the house. He knew exactly what he was doing. He held her hands that were zip tied behind her back with his left hand and said, "Down the stairs." She was scared to death, but she didn't want to cry out since he had already threatened to cut her throat. *I just need to shut up and do what he says. Maybe I can get out of here in one piece with just a bloody nose*. He took her down to the basement and made her to stand facing him. He took off her belt, unbuttoned and unzipped her jeans. She thought, *oh my God, he's going to rape me*. He made her sit on the floor, he pulled her shoes off, pulled her jeans off and then pulled her panties off. She said, "Oh God, please don't rape me, don't, don't." Laughing he said, "The last thing I want to do is rape you, you disgust me."

He then stood her up, cut the zip tie, pulled off her shirt and her bra. She tried to make a move to get to the stairs but he was too fast. He grabbed her arm, swung her around and slapped her again. She stood completely naked in the middle of the basement. He said, "Careful, if I were you, I would not try anything like that again. Now lay down there on the floor on your stomach." She did as she was told. Then, he reached in his trousers and pulled out a parachute cord. He had her put her hands behind her back. He laced it around both of her wrists and tied a tight knot. He pulled both of her ankles folded up behind her buttocks. Tied those together and tied it to her wrists. She was completely hog-tied. Laying on the floor face down. She was unable to move her arms and legs. There was nothing she could do at this point. She couldn't fight back. She thought, *OK, go get money or jewelry and get out. Just take what you want and get out.* But she was afraid to say anything for fear of getting her throat cut. He reached into his other pocket, got a rag and jammed it into her mouth very tight. He took another rag placed it over her mouth and tied it around the back of her neck to keep her from getting the gag out.

Now, the killer had her just how he wanted her. She was helpless lying there on the cold basement floor. He started to get a sense of euphoria. He wanted to relish the moment. He didn't want to do anything. He just wanted to stand there and enjoy it. This vile nasty bitch. The one he had been thinking about killing for years was right in front of him finally. Minutes left for her life to be taken. He didn't want to rush things now, as this was extreme pleasure for him. After a full minute of silence, he decided that he needed to tell her what a rotten bitch she really was. He finally let out some of his deep seeded hatred for her. He told her she was a loathsome creature and she shouldn't even be allowed to walk the face of the earth. No, he said, she never deserved to live as long as she did. It was a crime on its face that she was the age that she was. She treated everyone she came across like a dog and thought she could get away with it. But now it was time to pay, wasn't it? Because Hell had just arrived at her front door. Yes, here he was, ready to dispense Hell's justice on her. She couldn't make a sound but her eyes were as wide as port holes. She was feverishly shaking her head no, and that just made him happier. "You don't want to die?" he asked as he relished her terror. He pulled up a chair to her and sat down.

"You think you have a right to live?" she nodded her head yes. "Do you think I'm here for just a robbery?" She nodded her head yes. "Well, you're wrong bitch. I'm here only to torture you. I don't want anything you have. I want to torture you and then I want to watch you die. You're going to die in a little while. But you're going to die slowly with a lot of pain." She frantically shook her head no and made guttural sounds deep from her throat. The gag was so tight, she could barely breathe. It won't matter. He said to her,

"Are you having trouble breathing? For as long as you are about to live it won't make any difference at all. So, don't let that stress you out. No need to have any anxiety about it at all."

She tried to wiggle around, she tried rolling onto her back, she tried crawling on the floor away from him, but there was nowhere to go. As much energy as she could get to shimmy away, it was just one step for him. He stepped over to the radio and turned on some music. He scrolled through some channels and finds, by chance, AC/DC's "Highway to Hell." "How perfect," he screeched! "Oh, maybe this is your favorite song?" he says mockingly. "It will be a good song to die to. Oh yeah, let's play this one. I bet you had a lot of happy times with this song when you were younger because you are such a BITCH. Perfect song for you tonight. You can go out listening to the sweet melody," he said. The killer danced all around the basement to the music, holding his arms as if he had an imaginary partner. The woman watched in absolute gripping terror, yet the killer wore a big smile.

She was in a panic now, she tried everything she could to get loose, to get away, to roll over. But nothing worked. He would just push her back down with his foot on her back. He was in complete control. She was frantic and wasn't able to do anything. He reached into his pants pocket and pulled out a loop of parachute cord. The cord was about 18 inches in diameter. He stepped over her, slipped the loop over her head and under her neck. He pulled up on his end of the cord around her neck, which would elevate her throat against the weight of her body. He kept his left foot on her buttocks so she couldn't try to turn over. With his right hand, he pulled up on the cord, it gouged deeply into her throat. The guttural noises she made were clear and this almost stopped her breathing. He held it for 15 to 20 seconds and then he would release it. She could get her breath only through her nose since her mouth was gagged. She got a little bit of relief, like throwing a toothpick to a drowning man. *Let her have it* he thought. *Let her have a little bit of relief.* "I'll let you have some relief. I'll let you catch your breath," he said. "Isn't that better now? Don't you feel more relaxed?" She nodded her head. Yes, yes! "Okay," he said. "Let's try that again." He pulled up on the parachute cord again against her throat with the weight of her body choking her. She was frantic. His foot on her buttocks kept her from being able to move. Then he released her again after 10 to 20 seconds. Almost fainting, almost passing out. But the killer was careful to make sure she didn't. He didn't want her to pass out. He didn't want her to die right away. She had to feel it, she had to suffer. He let her down. "How do you like the music?" he asked. "What a fun night. You and me together, isn't it wonderful?"

He pulled up on the cord again, and again, and again always releasing it after several seconds. Always holding her up a little longer each time and mocking her about the music, or a joke or how perfect life will be when she's gone. What a great day tomorrow was going to be, sunny and bright. How everything will be even more serene than usual. Because she wouldn't be here to see it, she will be the newest member in the cesspool of Hell.

Finally, he said to her, "Well, I think I have to go now. I really can't stay the whole night. I'm sure you'll understand. Of course, I can't leave you alive. That would be against the reason I came here and since you recognized my voice, I really have no choice. So, I'm going to have to kill you this time." She shook her head violently No, No! He said, "Well, I just have to. I can't leave you alive and I can't wait any longer. It's time, it's time that I say good-bye. So, this will be your final chance to have a little bit of air. Any last words?" he chuckled. "Oh, whoops, I am so sorry. I forgot there is a gag in your mouth. Well, nobody really wants to hear your bitching anyway. You've done it your whole life. Let's just save it for tomorrow with all your new friends." The killer then pulled up on the cord. Clenched his fist tightly, made his arm rigid. He was a very strong man. He had a life time of physical work; he was no slouch. He took both hands and pulled up strongly and firmly with a foot on the small of her back. He could hear her choking. He didn't release the cord this time. There was no gentleness, there was no relief, and there was no air. She was choking to death. As it got closer and closer, he raised his foot. He stood aside her, put his right foot right in the center of her back, right between her shoulder blades with his toes right at the base of her neck. He pulled up on the cord and pushed down on his foot at the same time. All the while he had a giant smile on his face. It seemed like a couple of minutes at least, but he wasn't about to let go. No, this was music to his soul. She was dying right now and he wanted to relish every minute of it. It's almost as if he couldn't let go, after three minutes he knew she was dead. But he thought, *I can't let go now. This feels too good.* He kept pulling up and pushing down nonstop. He probably held that position for a good five minutes, long after she had expired. Oh, what elation it was, euphoria for him, what a feeling of power. This was everything he had hoped for. This was exactly how he wanted it, exactly according to plan.

He dropped her face on the cold cement floor with a resounding thud. Blood smeared the floor from her bloody nose. *What a great night,* he thought. He reached down and slipped the garrote out from under her neck. He folded it up and put it in his pocket. "I can't leave this," he said. "This holds a lot of fond memories." He then gathered up her clothes, wadded them up real tight and put them in a small plastic grocery bag that he had brought with him and walked up the stairs from the basement. He turned the light out. *You don't want to waste electricity,* he thought. He shut the basement door. But then, he noticed the bloody footprints from the kitchen to the basement door where he had dragged the bitch earlier. "Ha, Ha," he laughed. "A clue. Well, won't that be nice for some mail order Inspector Clouseau to find? Maybe they'll realize it started in the kitchen and continued to the basement." He headed for the back door. He suddenly stopped, went to the living room and picked up her dog. When he got outside, he slit the dogs throat and threw it in the trash. Then he removed the surgical booties from his shoes to ensure he left no bloody trail. He put them in the bag with her clothes, walked through the yard and gathered up Whisper. Off he went down the alley out into the darkness. It was a long walk back to his car, but it was a quiet nice evening, with a fingernail moon and a mild breeze. There wasn't anybody out. He only passed one other person on the other side of the street walking a dog and that person paid absolutely no attention to him what so ever. They were busy on their phone. He made it back to his car. Got in, threw Whisper in the trunk and gave him a dog biscuit. He headed off down the road.

As he headed home, he knew he would have to make sure that he carefully hid the bloody clothes, his shoes, the garrote, the clown mask, the K-bar knife. He would need them all later. Half of his plan was in motion. He still had to make sure the person he planned on framing for the murder would eventually get his also. But that wouldn't happen right away, rather it would be some months down the road. Everything had to happen in due course. *Those who rush always fail, hurrying makes mistakes*, he thought. A man should never hurry and he didn't like people who did. As he drove, he couldn't help but get the thoughts about the night he just had out of his head. He didn't rape that horrible she-wolf. He couldn't have, he had no desire. The thought of having sex with her sent bile up to this throat. When planning the killing, he often thought about the ending. Now he's got his revenge. She had really suffered, and that put a huge smile on his face. She had gotten the pay back for all the awful things she had done in her life. All the ways she had mistreated everyone. Yes, she deserved all that and she did pay tonight. Probably, if the world was a fair place, that torture would have gone on for months. He had actually thought about that, but there were too many chances of getting caught. He would have to take her someplace else and do it, but logistics was just too much to plan. No, this was simpler, shorter, and easier. He remembered how he has always told himself that killing was easy but getting away with it was difficult. That was the key to his plan, to get away so he could savor it, relish it and enjoy the nightmare with its hydra heads and re-live it over and over. That's what he wanted to do; be unknown to everyone until they caught the killer, he laughed, then he could cherish it and watch the one he pinned the murder on have to suffer as well. Ah, sweet revenge on two people that he really hated. *What could be a better plan than that,* he thought.

Just then he passed a Tennessee Highway Patrol car parked in the middle of the interstate highway. *"Careful,"* he thought. *You still have evidence on you.*

You don't want to do anything stupid to call attention to yourself. Before he left his house, he made sure that all his blinkers, taillights and headlights worked. Everything was proper. Registration, tags, insurance, and everything was in order. He wanted no reason for the police to stop him. If he did get stopped, he knew he could talk his way out of it. As he passed the trooper, he watched intently in his rearview mirror. The trooper sat there, didn't move. "He's after speeders," the killer chuckled. "Yeah, you'll get some speeders tonight you asshole. That's all you're good for anyway. Catching speeders." The killer slipped into the dark night. He couldn't wait to get home. *He was going to have some pleasant dreams tonight,* he thought. Just re-living the dance in the basement to that beautiful song. When he was far away from the city so his I-phone could not be placed there that night, he clicked his I-phone on, hit Spotify, gave a voice command for a search of AC/DC "Highway to Hell," and it started playing. A giant smile came across his face as he started to hum along to the tune and drove into the dark Tennessee night. This was going to be his new favorite song.

Chapter Eight:
An Avenging Angel

Welding steel was one of Sparky's favorite things to do. He learned it as a kid growing up on a farm in rural East Tennessee, and he later joined the Navy and became an electrician. That's where his shipmates gave him the nickname, Sparky. He worked on all the electrical ship systems and had some surprisingly good skills. He was putting both of those skills to work today in his basement workshop in South Pittsburgh, in East Tennessee. Sparky was barely scraping by; he had a 23-year-old pick-up truck that was full of rust. He made some side money welding and he worked at a truck stop once in a while. He tried driving an Uber but he didn't like that at all. The people really annoyed him. Sparky liked things more than he liked people. *People were always problems* he thought. They are just walking negative particles. Steel and electrical wire, those are things you can do something with. Those things can't talk back to you. They are things that will perform as designed. Those are things that don't lie to you or cheat you or try to do you wrong.

Sparky was his own man but he was an angry man inside. He really didn't have any friends. He got a general discharge from the Navy because he was, at times, difficult with his Chief Petty Officer. He always wanted to argue about his assignments and how they should be done. After the Navy, he just kind of bounced around, went to Florida, then up to Virginia. He tried a job at a shipyard doing some welding but he didn't like that. The boss was too demanding and the work was long hours. Sparky wanted to impress everybody with his skills and if the people weren't impressed, he would decide to move along. He thought he could do better on his own but that hasn't proved to be financially sustainable for him.

But today he was in his element, he was welding a box. It was 16 inches long by 18 inches deep. It was rectangular in shape and it was open on one end. Sparky thought, *this will be just perfect*. It was exactly what he needed. After finishing the steel box, he moved over to his other bench full of his electrical supplies. He started soldering some wires together. Tack welding a battery case to a flat plate. Stringing some wires carefully, meticulously snipping them off, stripping the ends and soldering new connections. Sparky wanted everything to be perfect. Everything to function as designed. Just like he did aboard ship. No chances for error, no mistakes. Whatever Sparky made, it was going to work and work perfectly. There were no second chances on a ship's complicated electrical system for things to work correctly and Sparky put all of his skills to the test this morning in his basement.

The switch he was wiring in was an unusual one. It worked off of a remote-control. He had gone to the

Hobby Lobby in Chattanooga and bought a remote-control model airplane transceiver and receivers. The receivers were small and they just worked the wing flaps on the model airplane. They turned a round disc on top of a small box. They were called a Servo motor and were very small. Sparky was soldering wires so that a switch would make a connection causing the Servo motor to turn. Of course, he could turn it remotely with his transceiver from afar. The range on this model was about a mile. The more Sparky worked, the happier he got. A smile came over his face. He wasn't his usual angry self, no, he was enjoying this. This was going to be something that he was really, really going to relish. Every second, every minute of making his creation made Sparky ever more elated. He hadn't felt like this since he was young when he was accomplishing something. Like when he played sports in South Georgia. He was on the football team and he did pretty good. His brother was a great athlete and he was much better than him. Sparky idolized his brother who later went on to play football in college at the University of Georgia and was a tight end. Sparky always looked up to him. Sparky's parents had been divorced when they were young and since his dad was not around, it was his big brother he admired. Two years older, bigger, stronger, more adept at athletics. Yes, his older brother was his hero in everything he did. Today was for his older brother and he was going to find out how much he really loved him. With the Servo motors in place on the metal plate Sparky had fashioned, the battery pack was in place and the wires soldered down. It was time to test his contraption. Sparky rigged a light bulb to the two switch contacts. He also wired in a buzzer, but that was going to be for another switch he was going to include. Sparky went outside with his transceiver and stood about 50 feet away from the basement door and he hit the remote-control lever on his transceiver box. He could look through the door and see his contraption sitting on his work bench. The light lit and the buzzer sounded. *Perfect circuit*, thought Sparky. It functioned as intended.

The next test would be for distance. Sparky took the plate, walked it as far away as he could on his property all the way to the tree line. It was about a half mile. *That will be a good test,* Sparky thought. This transceiver is supposed to reach about a mile. He walked away from the shed to the tree line and sat the contraption on a tree stump, and then he walked all the way back to his shop. Sparky could see the tree stump along the dark tree line. It was dusk and the light was just low enough that he was able to make out a light bulb if it worked correctly. He hit the transceiver, sure enough, he saw the light. He could even hear the buzzer in the quiet Tennessee evening. *Perfect,* he thought. The range is good too. He went back and retrieved his device, laid it back on the workbench, went upstairs, opened the frig and got out a Pabst Blue Ribbon, sat in his lazy-boy chair and turned on the news. *Let's see what the God damn politicians have screwed up today,* he thought. The news just made him more and more angry the longer he sat there. The whole country was a putrid place, *a bottomless toilet swirling with shit* he thought. After two more beers he crawled into his bed. He had to get up early as he had a welding job tomorrow and he needed the money. When Sparky got up the next morning, it was drizzling in East Tennessee. As he got in his rusty pick-up truck and headed out to his job, he thought, *it'll be soon, it'll be very soon.* No one is going to do that to my brother, no one at all. *Judgement day is coming and it can't come soon enough,* thought Sparky.

Chapter Nine:
Is This Justice?

Eleanor loved living on the lake. It was such a beautiful setting. When the morning sun came up, they could sit out on the front porch and watch the sunrise. *It never got old* she thought. The rising sun had a freshness to it. The thought of a new beginning, a new day, a new challenge. Learning something new was just stimulating to her in every regard. Eleanor and Barry lived on a body of water in Northern Alabama just below the Tennessee state line. It was actually the Tennessee River but it looked like a lake and it bent around to the northwest up into Tennessee and Kentucky through a beautiful area called "The Land Between the Lakes." It dipped down to Florence Alabama, from there, back across Northern Alabama to Scottsboro and up into Eastern Tennessee where it formed the Tennessee Valley. It was a naturally beautiful region of the country with mild winters and warm climate. Not too densely populated but certainly modern and she just loved living there on the water.

Her husband, Barry, was an avid fisherman. He would fish at every chance he got and this morning was his semi-annual fishing trip with her sister's husband from Nashville. They were fishing buddies. Always on the phone. That's all they ever talked about. Lures, fishing poles, fish finders, boats, where to find the best fish, who caught the biggest bass, what should they try for next, fishing gear, fishing clothes, fishing talk, fish, fish, fish, etc. These two guys loved fishing more than anything in the world. Barry loved fishing more than he loved Eleanor, he would say, and she would laugh about it. Well, Eleanor would take second to the fish. Barry was a pretty good husband. He provided for her and he worked hard. They were able to get this beautiful home on the lake with the most serene setting. Barry was a good man; he had his faults like everybody else but he took very good care of Eleanor and they had been married for 17 years. This Saturday morning, she had risen early. She was making breakfast for Barry and her sister's husband who had come down from Nashville last night. He got in late. She was excited to get them going out on the boat and on their way. Once they had finished their breakfast, she was free to leave and headed up to Nashville for her own semi-annual shopping trip with her sister. Eleanor had made the guys a hardy country breakfast; salted country ham, scrambled eggs, biscuits with homemade jam and some home fried potatoes. The guys loved it. They drank copious amounts of coffee and laughed, and talked about their upcoming fishing adventure. Eleanor left nothing to chance. She also had packed them a big lunch of sandwiches, chips, pickles, homemade chocolate chip cookies, cold drinks, etc. She knew they would be out on the boat all day. Normally, they came home at early evening with their catch, cleaned it on the back porch and threw it on the grill and fired it up. That's when they would crack a few beers and sit out and watch the sunset. Eleanor left them all the side dishes they'd need for their fish dinner so that it was easy to prepare. The house was clean, clean bedding on the spare bed for her brother-in-law. The guys were going to enjoy a weekend of fishing with no worries and Eleanor was going to enjoy shopping with her sister as well. Once the men had finished their breakfast, they grabbed their fishing tackle and headed to the boat dock at the edge of the property. The smiles on their faces were as big and bright as the Alabama dawn. They were in their happy moment. Eleanor just loved seeing Barry and her brother-in-law like this.

Once they fired up the outboard and were out of sight, Eleanor knew it was time for her to get on the road. She had packed the night before. She went to the bathroom and got ready for the day. She brushed her teeth, put on some make-up, grabbed her bag, and headed out the front door. She jumped in her little SUV and headed north. A lot of people couldn't get along with her sister because she had such an acerbic personality. It grated on many but since it was her sister, she had learned how to let it roll off her back. Sure, she could be bitchy at times and hard to get along with, but it always went away and so she didn't think a whole lot about it. Eleanor enjoyed the drive up the highway, passing the sights and watching the beautiful scenery go by. She traveled through Lawrenceburg, TN, watching all the Amish horse and buggies on the road. *Interesting people, but how can you live in such primitive conditions,* she thought. No matter what, they seemed to love their life and there was a fair number of them in this particular area. They had a whole colony. There were Amish shops on the sides of the roads. With whole families selling homemade baskets, wooden furniture, jams, breads, and canned goods. Eleanor would sometimes stop and shop to see if there was anything that tripped her trigger. She wasn't in a hurry to get to Nashville. Their shopping trip wouldn't start until the afternoon and would go into the evening. So, they would dinner out. By late morning, Eleanor was close to her sister's house and winding through the neighborhood streets in Hermitage, which was a section of Nashville. Small neat houses in a row, sidewalks, and huge shade trees marked this well-established neighborhood where her sister had lived for the past nine years. Eleanor always enjoyed coming to Nashville. It had a little vibe about it; all the country music and the country stars, the tall buildings downtown, etc. They didn't have that in her section of Florence, Alabama. The highest building was only a few stories. It was a tiny town compared to Nashville and she liked the feel of the city for a change. She pulled into the driveway and saw her sister's car and knew that her sister was probably all ready to go. *I can't wait to see her; she's going to love the little gift I got her. I know she will really appreciate it,* she thought. Eleanor got her sister her favorite perfume from Macy's Department store. She had the gift wrapped and was anxious to give it to her to start off their visit.

With the gift in her purse and just one small overnight bag in hand, she walked up to the front porch and rang the bell. She waited a minute but her sister didn't come to the door. *Maybe she's in the shower, I'll ring again,* Eleanor thought. She rang the bell again and again, nothing. *Well, let me look in the window,* she looked in through the front window on the porch into the living room. She didn't see anybody and everything seemed quiet. Her car was in the driveway so she has to be here. It seems odd since she hadn't heard her sister's dog. That dog would always know if anyone even stepped on the front porch and would start yapping like crazy. *Maybe she's is out around the back,* thought Eleanor. *She could be out in the garden, back by the garage, taking the dog out to go to the bathroom before they left.* She decided to walk around the back of the house, but didn't see her sister anywhere in the back yard. She walked up the small stoop and knocked loudly on the back door. Again, no answer. She called out for her sister several times all the while knocking. Nothing. By now Eleanor was thinking her sister is just not hearing her for some reason. *Is she in the bathroom with the shower on*? She shouldn't be since she is very aware of what time she was getting there. *Is she messing around in the basement with something?* Eleanor couldn't figure out what was going on. *Could she be at the next-door neighbors? Her car is here so she can't be too far away.* So many thoughts kept running through her mind.

She could see inside the kitchen from a window in the back of the house. She had to lean over the back-porch railing to get a good view. When she looked in the window, she was shocked. She saw some broken dishes on the kitchen floor and what appeared to be blood stains. *Oh My God*, she thought. Her sister must be hurt or in trouble. *What's going on?* Eleanor started pulling on the door and yelling for her sister. The door was locked solid. She stepped across the porch and leaned over as far as she could. She pulled the screen off the window but it was locked as well. She ran down to the patio and picked up a small metal end table that had three steel legs on it. She carried it up and with one of the legs, she busted the pane of glass right above the lock on the double hung kitchen window. She smashed the glass, reached in and turned the latch and forced the window open. It wasn't easy to do but she knew her sister was in trouble and needed help. Eleanor had to clear any broken glass to make sure she wouldn't get cut and painstakingly climbed in through the window. She carefully got one foot in, stretched over from the porch rail, and got the other foot in while almost falling down on the kitchen floor as she entered. Once in, she screamed for her sister over and over with no response. She ran from the kitchen into the living room. Eleanor thought, *she's got to be here, how badly is she hurt? Is she upstairs laying down, did she go to the neighbors for help?* She frantically ran upstairs continually calling her sister's name. She ran into every bedroom, flung open all the closet doors, she ran into the bathroom, slid back the shower curtain. There was no one here. *Where could she possibly be? What should I do?* She needed to call Barry and her-brother-in law, so she ran back to the kitchen to where she saw the bloody smudges. The kitchen counter had blood on it, there were broken dishes on the floor and there was a trail of blood and blood smeared all over the floor leading to the basement door. Eleanor had been in the house many times and she clearly knew it was the basement. She was in a state of near panic when she grabbed the basement doorknob. She flung it open so hard that it slammed against the wall and she whisked herself down the stairs. As she turned at the bottom of the stairs, the sight of horror knocked her back. It was as if she was hit in the chest with a flat head shovel when she saw a naked woman lying on her stomach, legs hog-tied behind her back. Her sandy hair was a total mess. It was clearly her sister. She was so frightened; she could barely move and didn't know what to do. At first, she hesitated because the sight was so unbelievable and shocking. But then she thought, *I have check her, maybe she is still alive.* She quickly ran over, placed her hand on her sister's throat, closed her eyes and felt for a pulse. She was scared, she was scared down to her marrow but she had to do this. *Is her sister OK? Is her sister alive?* Eleanor could feel no pulse. She put her hand in front of her mouth, she could feel no breath. *Oh My God! She's Dead*, Eleanor thought. She took a deep breath and ran frantically up the stairs. She went out to the front porch, got her cell phone from her purse and dialed 911.

911 Dispatch asked, "What is your emergency?"

Eleanor replied, "My sister has been attacked. I think she's dead, maybe. She's tied up in her basement. Please, send help right away."

911 Dispatch said, "Okay Ma'am, give me the address and I will get help on the way and tell me your name."

Eleanor quickly provided the address and gave them her name as she breathed heavily into the telephone. The 911 operator asked Eleanor if she was OK. "Yes, just petrified," she said.

911 Dispatch asked, "Do you know if anyone else is nearby? Are you inside the home? "

Eleanor replied, "I'm on the front porch."

911 Dispatch said, "I want you to walk to the neighbor's house. Either next door or across the street. You can communicate with the neighbor if you want but I need you to be in sight when the first police car arrives. Do you understand?"

Eleanor responded, "Yes, yes, I'll do that right now."

911 Dispatch said, "I need you to stay on the phone with me until I can get you in contact with the first team of officers who arrive."

Eleanor said, "Yes, thank you, thank you."

Within just a few moments she could hear the sirens. The number of sirens seemed to increase. First to arrive was a Metropolitan Nashville police car. Lights flashing, siren blaring the officer roared up to the residence. Metro Police was written on the side of the cruiser and on the trunk, it said "Nashville's Guardians." Another car came from the other direction. Eleanor rushed down from the neighbor's porch across the street where she had rung the bell and quickly aroused the neighbor.

"My sister has been hurt, killed maybe. She's in the basement," she said to the officer.

"OK," the officer said. "You just wait here. Did you see anybody else inside? Did you hear anybody moving around inside?"

"No, I didn't see or hear anybody in the house," she said.

"OK, we'll go in and take a look, I want you to stay right here," the officer emphasized.

Two Metro Police Officers drew their sidearms and proceeded up the front porch into the house. As they moved in, they yelled "Metro Police, come out with your hands up. Metro Police." As they moved through the house quickly, they saw the blood in the kitchen. One officer quickly went upstairs for a security sweep. The other officer went to the basement where the witness reported where she found the victim. The officers did this sweep extremely quickly so they could render aid to the victim. They had to do a quick search for anyone else in the home, they couldn't have anyone shooting down their backs. They had no idea what was going on in the house and before they could render any aide, they had to make sure that officers or any paramedic attending the victim were not going to get assaulted either. They completed their task in a few minutes. The officer from upstairs came down to the basement. They saw the victim hog-tied, naked on the basement floor. The first patrol officer took her pulse but he could clearly see she was deceased. He had been an officer for eight years and he has seen many dead bodies. They had a certain look, a certain coldness, a blueness to the skin. The first signs of post mortem lividity. He knew they had a homicide. The officer says, "OK, let's go outside on the porch, let's get homicide in here and let's get this scene secured but we may have to get a paramedic here just to do a quick back-up of our diagnosis."

As the officers walked out to the porch, A Metro Fire Engine Company had arrived, the firefighters were walking up to the porch with their paramedic gear. "Hey guys," the first officer said. "We clearly have a deceased victim in here. So, let's just take one of you to come in, verify no pulse, verify no breathing and then we can preserve this crime scene so we don't have everybody tramping around in there."

"OK, we'll do," said the captain.

They picked one of the paramedics. "Watch where you step," said the patrol officer. "We have to keep the scene right." They quickly stepped down to the basement. He let the paramedic examine the body. The fire department paramedic said, "You are clearly correct, she is deceased. No need to move anything, she's been dead for some time."

"OK thanks," said the officer. "Let's get out of here quick. homicide gets really particular on these scenes". "Got it," the paramedic said. They moved up the stairs went outside and with two other officers waiting on the front porch.

The sergeant arrived; he asked them what they had. They described the victim in the basement. The blood in the kitchen, and the broken dishes. "We best just wait for homicide," the sergeant said. "Those boys get their undies in a Gordian knot if we breathe on anything and I lost all my curiosity years ago. I don't have that urge anymore." The three officers looked at each other and said, "Yeah, we're getting that way too sarge and we don't even know what a Gordian knot is."

Within minutes an unmarked car pulled up. Then another and another. Two metro homicide officers walked up, waved to the uniformed officers. "What have you got?" The patrol officer described the scene, and what they had done. They told them how they had allowed only one paramedic in to check for vitals. "She is clearly deceased. She is the owner of the house. That's her sister right there sitting in the back seat of the radio car. Her name is Eleanor."

The homicide officer said, "OK, thanks guys, just stay out here with us as we are going to have a whole forensics team here. sarge, can we keep your guys for a little while?"

The sergeant replied, "Yeah, if you have to, I understand."

The homicide officer said, "Do you have anybody else you can give us to do a neighborhood check?'

The sergeant replied, "I can give you two more officers and we can collapse some of the zones, I'll see what I can do."

The homicide officer said, "Thanks, we have more detectives coming as well. We need to do a good neighborhood canvas while everything is fresh."

"Right," said the sergeant. "I'll get you a couple of guys here shortly."

"Thanks sergeant," the homicide officer finished.

Just then, the metro crime scene van pulled up and two crime scene technicians got out. They waved at homicide, they went around to the back and got some of their briefcases and walked up the deck. "What does it look like?" asked the forensic technician. "Female, white, victim, hog-tied in the basement according to the first patrol officer," said the homicide detective. "We were just about to go in, but since you're here, let's all go in together real slow."

"You got it," said the tech. As they entered, in a single line, there were two forensics technicians and the two homicide detectives. The patrol officers were ordered to stay on the porch and to just hold everything real close. One of the crime scene technicians had a camera and a video camera strapped around her shoulders. As they walked in, she took pictures of the scene and a video as they entered into the basement as it would all be necessary for the criminal case if there was one. *Sometimes there was and sometimes there wasn't,* she thought. Sometimes the killer is already dead, sometimes the killer never gets caught. Sometimes it is suicide. But nevertheless, they have to record and prepare like there is going to be a trial. Violent death is always serious business, as serious as a heart attack.

The detectives did a quick look around with their flashlights. They didn't touch any of the existing lights switches because forensics was going to have to fingerprint everything. They put on their little crime scene booties before they entered the house so they would not contaminate the crime scene. They were as careful as they could be but you have to enter the scene. You can't investigate if you can't get in there and they had to look it over. The basement looked fairly normal. There was a chair pulled over, very close to the body. A radio was on playing a local station. Apparently, the killer had been sitting next to the victim at some point. The cause of death was not immediately apparent but it did look like there were marks on her neck. She was face down and they didn't want to move the body too much until everything was photographed. They will take a close look at her face, they will look inside her mouth, roll her over to look for other signs of wounds but everything had to be photographed exactly how she was found first.

They had called for the medical examiner to come by. They wanted a representative from that office on scene whenever there was a homicide like this. One that is so brutal and so deliberate. This wasn't some accidental domestic case obviously. They don't know who killed her but whoever did, he or she or they really had a purpose. They didn't know what it was. They didn't know if it was robbery or passion, or even a serial killer. You had to be prepared for every strange turn this case might take. About 20 minutes later a representative from the medical examiner's office arrived. Forensics had taken all the pictures of the body that they needed. Dusted for fingerprints around the basement areas, light switches and so forth. They waited for the permission of the medical examiner to cut the parachute cord loose from the body and turn the victim over.

As they did this, the detectives clearly wanted to get good photographs of the knots used to tie the feet and ankles together. Sometimes the knot can be critical evidence. The ends of the rope appeared to be parachute type. The cord was drab olive green and thin. Could be key evidence as well. Anything to do with the cord might help them catch the killer. They cut the cord around the wrists and ankles and left the knots intact. They could then roll the body over to examine for gunshot or knife wounds, bruising, and strangulation marks. On the victim's neck, they saw multiple lines indicating strangulation attempts. The coroner said, "Wow guys, there's not one mark but multiple marks. We'll just have to see what the cause of death is. It looks like there have been a lot of strangulation attempts and maybe strangulation is the cause of death since we don't see any other wounds. No gunshot or stab wounds or apparent blunt force other than a bloody nose. But it's too preliminary to know for sure. We have got to get to the windpipe and take a look and see if it's been crushed."

The detective said, "Right, pretty gruesome looking method. She would be helpless in that position. It wouldn't be hard to strangle someone like that."

The Medical Examiner replied, "No Sir, it wouldn't. Once you have somebody tied like that, you have complete control. They are at the total mercy of the killer. If they have no plans on letting you go. It's going to be your demise for sure." The detectives then went upstairs as forensics was in the kitchen finishing up the photography, picking up the dishes. The lead technician called the detectives to the kitchen counter. "Look at this," he says. "We have already photographed it."

Scrawled on the white countertop in blood were two letters. The technician says, "We discovered this under a plate of cookies. It appears to us like the victim may have scrawled the letters and then pulled the plate of cookies on top to hide them. However, it happened, it happened during the assault." The detectives watched carefully from the side until forensics was done and then they moved around themselves looking at address books, and making note of what was on the counter. Looking for anything out of place. "Where is the husband or man of the house?"

one detective said to the other. "Not sure yet since we haven't talked to the witness. The sister of the victim. She is in the back of a radio car."

"Right, why don't we do that first? While we are doing that, forensics can sweep the upstairs and then we can go back in and take a look."

"OK, sounds good."

They stepped outside to the radio car and they interviewed Eleanor. Eleanor relayed to the detectives that the victim was her sister and her husband had gone to her house in Florence Alabama for the semi-annual fishing trip with her husband, Barry. She told them that when her brother-in-law was at her place for the fishing weekend, she would always come up to Nashville and spend the weekend shopping with her sister. That she had left this morning after making breakfast for the guys and what time she had arrived. She described everything about finding her sister's body in the basement. The detectives asked her questions about when her brother-in-law got to her house? How did he seem? Did everything appear normal? Was he acting any different than what she knows about him? Did she sense a red flag about his body language? Eleanor replied, "No, everything seemed normal. The last time I talked to my sister was Friday afternoon when we were planning our shopping trip for Saturday. My sister said her husband was all ready to go, he had all his fishing gear packed. He was looking forward to the trip. Everything seemed normal. My sister didn't say anything was wrong or that they had a fight and I got no ill feeling that anything was going on with them. I need to call Barry but the guys turn off their cell phones when they go fishing. They don't want to be bothered by anything or anybody. They just want to be away from all that stuff."

The detective asked, "So, where are they now?"

Eleanor replied, "They are out on the Tennessee River fishing.

They won't be back until evening when they come home to

cook their catch for dinner."

The detective asked, "What time do you think you can reach him by phone?"

Eleanor replied, "Probably around seven o'clock."

The detective said, "Alright, well we would like to get his cell number as well so we can give him a call."

Eleanor said, "OK, sure."

She gave the detective Barry's cell phone number.

Just before the detectives walked away from Eleanor, they told her they would be in touch and asked her where she was going after this?

Eleanor replied, "Well, I don't know, I'm too shaken up to drive home. I don't know what to do. I haven't even thought about it."

The detective asked, "Do you know anybody else here in Nashville you could stay with?"

Eleanor replied, "There is a woman I used to work with that lives about three blocks from here. Her name is Delores and I'll give her a call and see if I can

spend the night with her." The detective said, "That would be great. I'm sure your brother-in-
law will be rushing home this evening anyway when he hears the news and by that time the crime scene will be released and we will want to talk to him as well."

Eleanor said, "Thank you Officers."

The two detectives walked away from her to go back inside the house. "How do you want to handle it?" one of them said. "I think we should call down to Florence PD in Alabama and get a couple of their detectives to be waiting at the house when the guys return to the dock from fishing. They can be the first to tell them and watch their reaction in person. We can give them some preliminary questions. Let them make the observations for us and then they can put the husband on the phone to us."

"That sounds like a good plan. Hearing him and not seeing him is kind of weak at the moment."

"Correct, by the time we get down there it'll be too late, better to let the Florence PD do it."

"I agree. Let's go up inside the house and take a quick swing around before we go back to the squad room."

"OK."

The two detectives walked back in the house; forensics was finishing with the upstairs just as they came in.

"Anything upstairs?" one of the detectives asked.

Forensics tech said, "Nothing disturbed, no blood, nothing has been ransacked. Looks like everything we saw; the crime was in the kitchen and the basement. But we did take a bunch of photographs. We got everything videotaped as well so it's all yours." The detective said, "Thanks guys."

"We'll file our report when we get back to the office, we should have everything typed up and in your box Monday Morning," said the crime scene technician as they walked away.

The detective said, "Thanks again."

The detectives did a sweep of the upstairs of the house but it was uneventful. As they came back downstairs, the medical examiner's office was loading the body on a gurney and taking it out the front door down to the mortuary wagon. Neighbors had gathered in the street and uniform patrol officers and plain clothes officers were interviewing the neighbors. The detectives were taking it all in. This was a fresh scene. They didn't quite have a direction as of yet. They needed to nail down all the time lines of the husband. They couldn't find any forced entry. The back door was locked, the kitchen window was broken but they knew Eleanor had done that to gain entry when she saw the blood all over the kitchen floor. *No forced entry and a dead woman hog-tied on the basement floor,* they thought. "We need to talk to the husband as quick as we could. He's out of town," one detective said. "Is that because his fishing trip was his alibi?" another detective asked. "Who knows. We got a lot of work to do," another detective commented.

The detectives called the Florence AL Police Department and asked two detectives there to go and meet Barry and his brother-in-law at the boat dock at the house when the guys got back from fishing. They supplied them with the address and the detectives from Florence said they would head out. The Nashville detectives gave them about a dozen preliminary questions to ask. Told them what they had. The severity of the crime and the time frame. They wanted them to make observations of the husband when he was interviewed and then to put the husband on the phone with the Metro Nashville homicide detectives. Florence PD was great, they told Metro Homicide, "We'll take care of it all. No problem".

"We'll call you this evening and keep you updated. We'll see what we can do." The Florence detectives went and waited at the boat dock around 6:30 pm. About 15 minutes later, the bass boat came back with the two men in it. They watched it dock. As it did, they got out of their unmarked car and walked up to the boat dock. The two men in the boat saw them, looked at them and waved. The officers waved back. The lake was always a friendly place. Nobody seemed to get too upset about anything. This was an interview about a homicide and it was also a death notification. The husband couldn't be reached by phone so it was possible he had no clue that his wife has been murdered. If he did kill her, they wanted to watch his reaction very closely. The two detectives walked up

and flashed their badges- "Florence PD detectives."
They said, "Are you Eleanor's brother-in-law from
Nashville?"

"Yes, that's me," Eleanor's brother-in-law responded.
The detective said, "Can we talk to you in private for
a few minutes?"

Eleanor's brother-in-law asked, "What's this about?"

The detectives said, "Well, just walk over with us for
a few minutes." As they walked down the dock, he
left Barry standing by the boat.

He said, "Barry, it's OK, just let me find out what's
going on."

As they walked over to the grassy area just off the
dock, the detective said, "I'm sorry to inform you that
your wife has been found deceased at your home in
Nashville."

"WHAT? What do you mean deceased? I just left her
last night and she was fine. She was getting ready for
her shopping trip with Eleanor how can she be
deceased? What happened? What happened?" he said
in total shock.

The detective said, "Well sir, apparently she was
murdered."

He said, this time in a high tone, "MURDERED,
that's not possible. You must have the wrong house.
My wife wasn't murdered."

The detective said, "I'm sorry sir but it is the right
house, we were on the phone with Metro Nashville
homicide detectives this afternoon and we have a
couple of questions we have to ask you."

He said, still in shock, "Oh My God, I cannot believe this! I can't believe this is true. It can't be true."

"It's true," the officer said.

The detectives observed that the husband was animated and nervous, he was moving his arms, they felt that he was not as excited as anyone would be when given a death notice of that magnitude. Normally it hits one hard like an NFL middle linebacker sacking a quarterback. The detectives had seen it all before. They were watchful, was his reaction real? or was it Memorex?

He looked at Barry and yelled, "My wife has been found dead." Barry raced over. One of the detectives took Barry by the arm and said, "Can we talk to the husband alone just for a few minutes? I promise you it won't take that long. We'll stand right here."

"OK, OK, I'll just wait right here," Barry said.

The detective said, "Thank you sir."

The detectives started questioning what time the husband left Nashville, the relationship with his wife, anything that might have gone wrong, were they fighting? Was the marriage, OK? What time did he arrive at Barry and Eleanor's house? They carefully observed all of his reactions. They checked his arms and his hands. They asked to see his neck. They couldn't find any scratches anywhere on his face, neck or hands. No blood anywhere. He was clearly upset and animated but they couldn't really tell what that meant. They asked all the questions the Nashville detectives had provided and then they said, "OK, let's walk up to the porch." As they walked up to the back porch of the house, one of the detectives said, "Let's sit here."

"We want to put you on the phone with Metro Nashville homicide. Do you have a phone here?" said another detective.

"Yes, detective," he replied.

"Can you get it?" the detective asked.

He had his phone on him, it was just turned off. He reached into his pocket and retrieved it. The officer took the phone and dialed the Metro Nashville Homicide Division. He put the Nashville detective on the phone with the husband. The one officer sat down with him as that conversation ensued, as the other officer walked down to the boat dock and interviewed Barry. After about 40 minutes, the husband handed his phone back to the Florence detective and said, "He wants to talk to you." The two detectives conversed about what had happened and agreed they were finished with the husband for now and they would talk later. The two detectives shook the hands of the two men, walked back to their car, and got in.

"What do you think?" one detective asked.

"I don't know, it was hard for me to get a read on him. He was pretty upset but there has got to be more information before we can make a determination," responded the other detective.

"Yeah, this may be a tough one for Metro Nashville. I really couldn't tell you one way or the other if this guy is a killer or a victim. Let's head back to the detective bureau and give the Nashville guys another call. I'm sure we'll be working on this through the rest of the week. Sounds like it was really brutal."

"Yeah, it really does."

As the Metro Nashville homicide detectives got ready to leave the crime scene, Eleanor came up to them and said, "My sister has a dog. A Yorkie. It's her baby and it's not anywhere. If that dog was here, it would be yapping nonstop." The two detectives looked at each other. They had already scanned the house and found no dog. They decided to go around back and take a look. The back yard was very neat and well-kept so it would have been easy to see a small dog. They couldn't see anything. Just then one of the detectives lifted the lid on the trash bin and right inside the trash bin was a small yorkie dog. Blood everywhere.

The detective said, "Come look at this." The other detective peered into the trash bin and saw the dog and said, "Let's get a bag and get it out of there."

After the detectives walked around to the back of the house, Eleanor called her friend Delores. "Delores, it's Eleanor." Delores responded, "Oh hi Eleanor, what's going on. Haven't you gone shopping yet?"

"No, No, it's my sister," Eleanor said.

Delores asked, "What about your sister?"

Eleanor replied, "She's dead. She's been murdered."

Delores said in shock, "What?! Murdered? No, that can't be right!"

Eleanor said, "She's been murdered. I had to break into the house because she wouldn't answer and I found her in the basement. It's gruesome. I am too shaken up to drive home. Can I come and stay with you tonight?"

Delores said, "Of course, of course. Come on over. I'll be waiting." Delores hung up the phone. Panic started to set in. Oh no. What has happened. This can't be real. They had discussed how things were going to change once he got back from his fishing trip. Surely, he didn't mean THIS... No, no way. This is not what he had in mind. Delores knows in her heart that this is not what was supposed to happen. Divorce, that's it. Divorce. She had to compose herself. She had to look around to see if there are any remnants of their get togethers. Shirts left behind. Pictures laying around. Anything that would tie her to the victim or the victim's husband. This is how nightmares begin she thought. She was all scrambled up inside now. She was babbling to herself as she gathered the sheets to make up the bed in the guest room. *What just happened,* she thought?

Lonnie is manic now. He asked his brother-in-law to drive him the two hours to Nashville to meet with Metro homicide detectives. They packed up the car and headed out. Once they arrived in Nashville, they went by the house. There was a patrol car outside. The officer told them that they couldn't go inside, as it was still being held as a crime scene until it's released by detectives of the Homicide Bureau. Lonnie called the detective on his phone. The detective told Lonnie to come downtown to the Nashville Police Headquarters for an interview. Lonnie and his brother-in-law jumped in the car and drove to Nashville Police Headquarters where he was brought into an interrogation room by the homicide detectives. By now it's almost midnight. Lonnie was tired and his brother-in-law was made to wait outside the interview room. The detectives questioned Lonnie extensively. What time did he leave? Did he have a fight with his wife? What could have happened to her? Does he know what happened to her? Lonnie told the detectives that he wanted her dead many times but he denied killing her. The detectives pressed on an issue. "The coroner, they say, puts the time of death about when you left. All the doors were locked, no one else gained entry. The only person who forced entry was your sister-in-law, Eleanor." Lonnie said he couldn't explain it but he claimed he didn't kill his wife. The detective who had done extensive interviews throughout the neighborhood then braced Lonnie with the fact that he was having an affair with a neighbor named Delores. Lonnie sank in his chair; he wasn't expecting to be hit with that fact. He said, "Yes, he does love Delores."

The homicide detective said, "Delores has told us that you said it would all be over soon when you left for the lake and you two would be together. Is that true?"

Lonnie said, "Yes, it's true, but that doesn't mean I killed my wife."

The detective then asked Lonnie if anyone else had a key to his house.

Lonnie said, "No, just me and my wife. We are very private people."

The detective reached into his briefcase and pulled out an 8x10 photograph and laid it on the table in front of Lonnie.

"What's this?" Lonnie asked.

The detective said, "Your wife scrawled this in her own blood on the kitchen counter during the murder."

Lonnie just stared at the photograph with the initials LM in scarlet red.

The detective said, "Can you explain why she scrawled your initials on the countertop while she was being murdered?"

Lonnie stood up abruptly, knocking over the chair he was sitting on and yelled, "God Damn It! I'm done talking to you. I want a lawyer."

The detective cracked, "You may need more than one."

The detectives ended the interview and told Lonnie to wait. They went outside and met with the sergeant. They had a discussion about the case. There was no forced entry into the house. No one else was in possession of a key. The time of death matched for when the husband left. The husband clearly hated his wife and he had made statements that he did indeed wish she was dead before. He told a lady in the neighborhood that he was having an affair with, it would all be over soon. His initials were scrawled on the kitchen counter by the victim in blood during the murder. The victim was clearly telling us who the killer was. The detectives felt like it was a strong circumstantial case on the husband and they want to book him. The sergeant said that they should call the District Attorney's office and hear what they would say. In a short while, after consulting with the District Attorney, the detective got a murder warrant for Lonnie. He was booked into Metro jail for the homicide of his wife.

Lonnie was held without bond and six months later, he faced a trial in criminal court in Nashville Tennessee. The jury convicted him of the murder of his wife and he was sentenced to Riverbend Maximum Security Prison in Nashville.

Before Lonnie was sent to prison, Delores paid him a visit in jail. When she saw him, she broke down in tears. Lonnie wanted to console her but they were not allowed any physical contact.

Delores said, "Lonnie, what is going on? What happened? You didn't do this. I know in my heart you didn't do this. Look me in the eye and tell me you didn't do this."

Lonnie replied, "What does it matter if I did or didn't? I could shout it from the rooftops. It's a done deal. I have been convicted. I am going to spend the rest of my life in prison."

Delores assured, "We will work something out."

Lonnie said, "STOP. I don't want you coming to see me in prison. I don't want you sitting at home worrying about me. I want you to move on. Start a new life. We cannot be together and I will NOT allow you to go down this path with me. If you show up at the prison, I will refuse to see you. Please, Delores, promise me you will forget about me, move on with your life and start over."

Delores just stared at Lonnie; she couldn't believe what he was saying. The life she was expecting with this man was over. There was nothing either one could do. She would live the rest of her life believing Lonnie was innocent of this charge. Lonnie got up and left the visiting area without saying another word to Delores. She sat there for what seemed like forever. She finally got up and walked to her car. When she got in the car and behind the wheel, she broke down again. She sobbed uncontrollably. She screamed at the top of her lungs with a resounding guttural ache, pounding the steering wheel so hard that she was shocked she didn't break it. Delores sat in her car and cried, and after a waterfall of tears she was exhausted and had no tears left. *How could things have gone so wrong?* she thought. She put her car in drive and slowly made her way home playing over and over in her head what Lonnie had said to her. After a few months of whispers and stares and being pointed at constantly, Delores sold her house and moved to North Carolina where her brother was living. Leaving Lonnie and Tennessee behind.

Chapter Ten:
To Be or Not to Be

There was a major explosion heard for blocks. Donnelly was in a morning meeting and Tomi was in her office at channel 4. It broke all over the police scanners and her editor, Lee Thompson, sent her out racing to the scene with her cameraman. The explosion was a car Bomb killing Judge John Moran near the Metro Courthouse. The Judge had arrived at a local coffee shop about 9:00 a.m., and when he stepped out of his car, a bomb went off and killed him.

Tomi learned a long time ago that if you wanted to be a good reporter you had to be tenacious. You could not back down. You certainly did not take attitude from anybody. She had her share of police chiefs and detectives warn her to back off, but she stood her ground. Sometimes she made enemies and frazzled some kilts, but more often she was able to get people to trust her, and she kept her sources confidential. Now, she was trying to figure out the best way to get around all the crime scene tape. She decided to keep a low profile and tried to become invisible. She had snuck around crime scenes before. Sometimes getting close enough to at least have a story to lead with and other times not so much. She didn't care if she got caught trying to get closer to the bombing scene. She was ready to do whatever it would take.

When Tomi got to the scene it was a madhouse. At first, she was too far away from the scene to make an assessment or really see what was going on. But she had an idea. She grabbed her cameraman and they sneaked around other reporters, firetrucks, and police cars. She was going to sneak around to a different side and see if she could get closer without being seen. As they got around the side of the building and were getting closer, Tomi made a bold move and slipped under the yellow tape. Just then, she was spotted by the man in charge. She had no idea who he was, he was off in the distance in a business suit pointing toward her and he directed an agent to escort her away from the area. She couldn't even get close enough before she got caught.

Special Agent Fuller said, "Excuse me, what do you think you are doing?"

Tomi responded, "I am Tomi Bardsley, NBC news here in Nashville."

Fuller said, "Ma'am, it doesn't matter who you are or who you're with. The Special Agent in Charge has ordered me to remove you from the crime scene."

Tomi asked, "Is that the Agent in charge in the suit?"

Fuller replied, "Yes."

Tomi requested, "Can I talk to him?"

Fuller responded, "Ma'am if you don't mind, we have more important things to do right now than to stop and talk to a reporter. The Special Agent in Charge will talk to all reporters when the time is right. Please get back under the tape and let us do our job."

She wanted to interview The Special Agent in Charge of the bombing. She was pretty sure he would say absolutely nothing. But nothing ventured means nothing gained. Tomi called her producer, Lee Thompson.

Tomi said, "Lee, who is this Special Agent in Charge of the bombing? I want to interview him."

Lee replied, "I doubt that he will meet with you. This is a fresh case, I'm sure they haven't even gotten any preliminary reports or findings. His name is Tim Donnelly and I've worked with him before, he is solid but he operates on Donnelly time, not on our deadlines."

Tomi said, "Lee, this is my first huge story since I've been in Nashville. I can't let another channel scoop me on this. You certainly don't want another channel to scoop us on this, do you? Don't you know anybody in his department who can get
 me an interview?"

She continued to hound him to make the call.

Lee responded, "I know the Special Agent in Charge, Donnelly. He is a great guy. Very relaxed, funny, very personable but if you want to get info from him you cannot be too aggressive. He's been doing this for years and he absolutely will not tell you anything. At least not now. Remember Donnelly time."

Tomi said, "Let me at least try. He can't be that rigid, can he?"

Lee responded, "You have no idea. Don't think because you are a woman that'll make a difference. Because it won't."

Tomi was well aware of how she looked. She was ethical and a pro. But hey, men were men and she did not have to hide the fact that she was a woman to be ethical. She has used her looks in the past to get into places she probably shouldn't have. She knew a smile, a tilt of her head, and slight lick of her lips could go a long way. She had no problem trying to use them on this particular Special Agent in Charge to get some information. She decided that dressing sexy couldn't hurt her chances. If he didn't give her anything she could run with, hopefully she got him to let his guard down and he'd give her dibs on any information.

Having been warned that Agent Donnelly was no one to be messed with, she had to feel him out, ask some personal questions but also play to his ego. She learned that to be in his position he would have to have a large ego. He kept his information close to the vest and would not reveal anything he felt would endanger the investigation.

Her producer was able to get her a one-on-one meeting with the Agent. Lee had asked Donnelly's Public Information Officer (PIO) for a quick interview. His newest reporter was new to the Nashville area and was hoping for a break. Donnelly reluctantly agreed. The PIO and Lee went back years so it was more of a favor. Donnelly told the PIO it was a waste of time and he didn't have anything to tell. He was going to Amerigo's restaurant off of West End Avenue for dinner and a drink. Tomi Bardsley can meet him there. Any time after 7:00 pm. Donnelly didn't have anything to tell this guy so the meeting shouldn't take very long.

Tomi walked into Amerigo's promptly at 7:01 and went straight to the bar. What a great place, small but chic. She had heard of Amerigo's but never had the time to go. As she continued to look around the room, she spotted him. She wondered if he realized she was the one he spotted and got her booted from the crime scene. This probably isn't going to go down well. Even though he was sitting down, she could tell he was tall. Very lean built but also very strong. His hair was just starting to gray in some spots. He was incredibly handsome. So much so it caught her off guard. He had a few years on her but she could tell his chosen career had given him a strong sturdy stature and you could feel the confidence he exuded. He was laughing and joking with the bartender. He didn't seem as intense as she thought he would be. It was clear he was a regular at Amerigo's and knew the bartenders personally. As she was walking toward him, Donnelly spotted the guy in front of her.

Donnelly asked, "You Bardsley?"

The gentleman said, "No sir."

Tomi peeked around the gentleman in front of her and said, "I'm Tomi Bardsley."

Donnelly said surprised, "You? You're Tomi Bardsley? I've seen you before. Ahh. you're the one who was trying to sneak closer to the crime scene and possibly compromise the investigation. With all the things I need to do, to make sure the crime scene is preserved, everyone running around doing their job to secure the scene, you show up trying to sneak a closer peek?"

Tomi responded, "Yes sir, that would be me. I would like to apologize for that."

Donnelly replied, "Apologize? You want to apologize. Being a professional reporter, you should have known that was not going to get you anywhere. If you had gotten any closer, I could have had you thrown in jail to keep you out of my way. The last thing I needed was to take a busy agent and have him escort you away from the scene."

Tomi, knowing she had instantly gotten on the wrong side of this guy decided to switch tactics and totally ignore his irritation.

Tomi said, "Hello Special Agent Donnelly, it's nice to meet you. Thank you for agreeing to meet me on short notice. Can I buy you a drink?"

Donnelly just looked at her and said nothing. It had been a long day. He had nothing he could share and felt this meeting was a waste of time. He wanted a nice peaceful dinner and a drink. The next several days were going be hectic and he needed to keep his mind focused on the bombing, not some new reporter trying to make a name for herself. But hey, she is gorgeous so why not share a drink with a beautiful woman. Tomi grabbed the stool next to him and ordered a beer. She told the bartender to get him whatever he was drinking. She tried starting out with the professional BS trying to smooth him over. He saw right through it. She was now trying to formulate her next strategy but his intense stare on every part of her body was clogging her brain.

Tomi said, "Again I want to apologize for my antics this morning. Being a crime reporter, I wouldn't be doing my job if I didn't at least try. You would understand that."

Donnelly replied, "If doing your job means possibly compromising a crime scene then, yes, you were doing your job. You have some moxie; I will give you that. I have dealt with reporters my entire career. I have done more than my share of press conferences. At this point there just isn't anything I can share with you. It's too early in the investigation for me to give out anything."

Tomi requested, "Can you tell me anything about the bomb? What kind was it? What about the Judge? Any thoughts about who would want to kill him? Do you think there will be more bombs?"

Donnelly replied, "I'm sorry. I don't have anything I can share."

Donnelly changed the subject and said, "I understand you're new to Nashville. Where did you come from?"

Tomi replied, "New Jersey."

Donnelly asked, "New Jersey? What brought you to Nashville?"

"Not wanting to relive New Jersey," Tomi says. "I needed a change of scenery."

Donnelly responded, "Well, New Jersey to Nashville is a change of scenery all right. Just so you know the only reason I decided to meet you is I'm friends with your boss. Lee helped us a few years back with an informant on a school bombing. Lee's a good guy. He trusts me and I trust him."

Tomi decided to go a different route since she now knows Agent Donnelly isn't going to tell her anything.

Tomi asked, "Agent Donnelly, how long have you been with the ATF?"

Donnelly responded, "18 years, I was a local cop in Florida for six years before that."

Tomi quizzed, "Has your career always been in Nashville?"

Donnelly replied, "No, I have served in Atlanta, Miami, Washington DC and Nashville as present post. But I will sometimes travel all over on case assignments."

Tomi added, "I would like to ask that when things progress, and you are able to talk about it. Can I be the first person you talk to?"

Donnelly replied, "Hmm, you sure have got some cajónes' I will keep you in mind."

Tomi said, "Well not exactly cajónes." They both smiled.

She was taken by him. Did he mean he would keep her in mind giving her the scoop first, or just keep her in mind. Then she realized that she doesn't even know if he's married. She was so focused on her story and how handsome and charming he was, she never noticed a ring. Which was unlike her. She wasn't even considering such things after losing Joel. Agent Donnelly was not the tough and rigid man she was prepared to meet. She immediately felt his strength and confidence in his ability to do his job. She also felt his sexual prowess that simmered under the surface. He knew she felt it and he made sure she was aware. The way he talked, the way he leaned in to talk to her. He looked directly into her eyes when he spoke and she could not turn away. He had piercing blue eyes and she felt them down to her socks when he looked at her. Was that her fear or attraction? She wasn't sure but either way it was power. She found her breathing becoming very shallow. She found him extremely sexual and she realized she should end the interview so she could get some air and clear her head. She needed to get out of the bar and into the fresh air.

Tomi finished her beer, and thanked Agent Donnelly for his time. He handed her his business card and she headed toward the door. The bartender looked at Donnelly and said, "Hey, isn't she the new reporter on Channel 4?"

Donnelly replied, "Apparently she is."

The bartender said, "She's Hot."

Donnelly responded, "Yeah, a lot of TV news reporters are."

Just as Tomi got to the door, Agent Fuller walked in. As they passed each other, Agent Fuller turned completely around to watch her walk out of the restaurant. As he sat down next to Donnelly he said, "Isn't she the reporter you had me remove from the bombing scene this morning?"

Donnelly replied, "Yeah, that's her."

Fuller continued, "Man, she's Hot!"

Donnelly said, "Relax Al, we got work to do, and don't you already have a girlfriend?"

Al said smiling, "Yeah, but I might need two."

Donnelly was not expecting a female reporter. When he was told Tomi, he assumed it was a young man, some snotnose kid that was going to get under his skin and be an outright pain. It was partly true though, as Tomi had gotten under his skin already. He intentionally leaned very close to see if he could shake her up a little bit. He was impressed she held her own and didn't move. She didn't even look away when he stared directly into her eyes. He noticed her breathing changed and became shallow. At this point, he knew he was getting to her. He was surprised she was not the angry pit-bull some reporters can be. She was kind, soft spoken, and apologetic for her trying to get closer to the bombing scene. He had to give her credit for that.

Donnelly watched through the windows of Amerigo's as Tomi walked up the street. She is tall and thin. The outfit she chose to wear for this meeting didn't go unnoticed. Tight white jeans that hugged her curves and fit her body perfectly. Her legs were so long it seemed like they went all the way to her neck. Her white jeans tucked into white cowboy boots and a pale green top highlighted her red hair. He was not the only man watching her through the windows. He was intrigued by this Tomi Bardsley.

After Tomi left the bar, Donnelly couldn't stop thinking about her. She left rather quickly but he knew why. He felt it too. She was a stunning woman. That long red Irish hair framed her thin face perfectly. Her dark brown eyes were unsettling. There wasn't much he could tell her at this time but he did say that if anything new came up that he could share, she would be the first one he called. He wanted another meeting with her even if he didn't have anything to tell her. She was new to Nashville and she would need someone to show her around. Who better than an ATF Agent?

Tomi was back at the TV station the next morning for an editorial meeting. Reporters called it that, but it was about news assignments of the day. Editors, reporters, producers, and staff.

Tomi laid out her meeting with Agent Donnelly to Lee. As Lee suspected Tomi got no information from Donnelly, he decided to let her figure that out for herself.

Tomi began, "Donnelly is very hard to read. I apologized for my antics in trying to get closer to the bombing and he clearly wasn't happy about it. I'm just doing my job. He didn't need to be so short with me. I bought him a beer to help smoothen things over. He accepted it but I'm not sure if it helped my case. I thought he was going to put me in his black book. Then he tries flirting with me? I was so shocked that I felt my barometer rising but I was able to tamp it down. What a jerk."

Lee responded, "Well Tomi, I did tell you, you weren't going to get anywhere with him."

Laughing, Lee added, "Though I am not surprised he started flirting with you. He likes to throw people off their game. Especially beautiful women."

Tomi said, "If I keep on him, gently, maybe he'll give me first dibs on any new information."

After the editorial meeting, Tomi and a female anchor named Natalya Bettings, and producer Diane Wirth were all huddled together. The topic of conversation was Tim Donnelly. Since Tomi was new to Nashville, they wanted to get her perspective on this hunky ATF Agent.

Natalya was a strikingly beautiful woman who anchored both the 6:00 p.m. and the 10 p.m. new hours.

Natalya said, "So you met Agent Donnelly? Oh my God, he is so Dreamy!"

Tomi responded, "Yes, I met him. I tried to get some information on the bombing but he was pretty tight lipped."

Natalya asked, "Did he ask you about me?"

Chuckling, Tomi said, "No. Why would he?"

Natalya said, "I met him after a press conference on a gun trafficking story."

Tomi replied, "OK, I'm not sure why he would ask me about you."

Diane said, "Natalya thinks every man who meets her wants to date her."

Tomi responded, "Oh, okay."

Smiling, Tomi said, "Well for all I know he could be married."

Natalya clarified, "No, he just broke up with Dawn Bennett the model, she moved to New York. So, he is available."

Now Tomi knew he is single but that does not mean he's available. If he was fresh out of a relationship, that doesn't mean he's emotionally available. She doesn't even know if she's emotionally available at this point in her life. But Tim Donnelly certainly was making it a challenge. She found him dreamy as well. Could she get close enough to figure him out?

Chapter Eleven:
Is It Real?

A few days after the bombing, Agent Donnelly still didn't have much information to pass along. Tomi really wanted to see him and needed a reason to reach out other than the bombing. She took a chance and gave him a call. As the phone started ringing, she had a strong urge to hang up. Just as she was about to do just that, Agent Donnelly answered the phone.

Donnelly said, "Tim Donnelly."

Tomi's breath caught in her throat and for a few seconds she wasn't able to talk.

Donnelly said, "Hello?"

Tomi responded, "Oh Sorry, (clears her throat) Agent Donnelly, it's Tomi Bardsley."

Donnelly said, "Well, hello Tomi Bardsley. How are things at Channel 4? Lee keeping you on your toes?"

Tomi replied, "Things are quite busy. Still waiting for something to break so the Special Agent in Charge can pass the information along to me. Wouldn't that be fun?"

Donnelly said, "Fun," then laughs, "I need some fun that's true. But right now, things are moving along. Nothing I can share yet but it's getting close. I will help you out if I can later Tomi. You are persistent, but professional. I respect that."

Tomi said, "Thanks Agent Donnelly, I am glad that you remember I have big cajónes'."

Donnelly laughed and said, "Oh, I remember what you have, Tomi. Anything else?"

There was a long pause in the conversation.

Donelly asked, "Ms. Bardsley, is there something else I can help you with?"

Tomi hesitated, "Actually, there is. My best friend Gemma Hughes is playing at The Local tonight and I was wondering if you would be interested in going to listen to her?"

Tomi could not believe she had just asked Agent Donnelly on a date!!

Donnelly responded grinning to himself, "Are you asking me out on a date?"

Tomi replied, "A date? Well, I hadn't really thought of it that way. My friend Gemma is a great singer and I just thought you'd like to go listen."

Donnelly said, "OK. Sure, I will go on a 'non-date' to listen to your friend Gemma. Can I pick you up or do you want to meet me there for this 'non-date?'"

Tomi was getting so flustered. Date, non-date. He is messing with her and she knew it.

Tomi said, "I'll meet you there. How about 9:00 pm?"

Donnelly replied, "I'll be there. By the way, do you know how to swing dance?"

Tomi responded, "Sorry, I do not."

Donnelly said, "No worries, I'll teach you. Make sure you wear some comfortable dancing shoes."

Tomi was not much of a dancer. She could barely keep time to any song let alone go out and dance where people could see what a mess she was. Agent Donnelly would be in for a surprise when she spends most of the time stepping on his feet.

She immediately called Gemma and told her about Agent Donnelly and what was going on. Gemma was very excited to have Tomi come and listen to her sing and to bring an ATF Special Agent with her. Gemma couldn't wait to see this Agent and see him and Tomi together. Tomi tried to play it off as no big deal but Gemma knew Tomi well enough to know this man has gotten under her skin. Gemma and Tomi discussed what Tomi should wear for maximum interest from Agent Donnelly.

Tomi decided on a pair of very fitted, boot cut blue jeans. Gemma talked her into getting a pair of cowboy boots. They're a must for Nashville. Tomi got the most subdued brown pair she could find. She did admit with the jeans, they looked awesome. She had a plain white button-down cotton shirt. She didn't want to appear overdressed, but she did make sure that her top was buttoned just above her breasts. You could see them but again not really, it depends on how she moved. She

thought about putting her hair up but decided against it.

She got to The Local about 20 minutes before Gemma was set to go on. They sat and had a quick drink and Gemma gave Tomi the third degree about Agent Donnelly. Again, Tomi told Gemma it was a work situation but Gemma and Tomi both knew that was a lie. They both just laughed about it.

At exactly 9:00 p.m., Agent Donnelly walked in the door. When she first met him, he was sitting down and she could tell he was tall but seeing him standing there, she didn't realize how tall he was. 6'2" or 6'3". He was dressed in jeans. No cowboy boots, dress shoes, pale blue button-down dress shirt; starched and well pressed so tight she was waiting for it to snap when he bent his arm. Even on a leisurely night out his dress was impeccable. It took him a second to spot her. As he was making his way through the bar, practically every person there stopped him and shook his hand. They had a laugh or a short conversation. The bartender knew exactly what he would be drinking and had it out and ready when he got to her table. She should have known he has been here several times. He bent over and told Tomi that he has a better place to sit.

He grabbed her hand and they went to sit at a high-top table, just left of the stage but closer to the dance floor. The place was busy but not packed. The Local was a unique Nashville place. It was far enough from the downtown excitement to be

just a cup of cool. It was owned by a song writer and its clientele was the cognoscenti of Nashville's musical scene. Tourists could be found there as well in small numbers pulled by the magnetism of The Music City, in a more subdued setting. The walls had several stained-glass pieces. One of a guitar, a saxophone, and a keyboard done in brilliant purple. There was even a stained-glass drum set on a shelf by the bar. Above the front door was a sign that says "Leave a Local". Tomi asked Tim about it. He told her it meant, come in as a tourist and leave as a local. The name fit the place perfectly. As they got settled, Donnelly asked Tomi what she would like to drink. She replied, "A Stella." When he came back with her drink, he sat so close to her that their legs touched. She was caught off guard but tried to not let him know that. He leaned in and said, "Cheers to great music." Tomi replied, "Absolutely." Tim leaned in and gently caressed her inner forearm. He was so close and he smelled amazing. Whatever cologne he was wearing took over all of her senses. Inside she felt a delicious flutter that unfurled the wings of her sexuality.

Gemma went on stage to start her show. She was an incredible singer and can sing whatever anybody asked her to. Four or five songs in she changed gears and started singing Mel Carter's "Hold Me, Thrill Me, Kiss Me", one of Tomi's favorites.

(Tomi and Joel used to dance to this in their living room. After Joel's death, Tomi would dance alone in her living room and weep). Agent Donnelly grabbed her hand and said, "Let's go." Tomi hesitated as it brought back strong memories of Joel.

"I'm not much of a dancer," she said.

"I'll lead, you follow," Donnelly replied.

He pulled her on the dance floor, grabbed her hand and held her so tight that she had no choice but to move where he wanted her to. Her head fit perfectly into his collar bone and she couldn't help but lay her head down and lean in.

His dancing was so slow and rhymical. He had his hand on the small of her back and he held her so close that every part of their bodies were touching. Tomi could barely breathe. When the song was done, Donnelly didn't let go. He looked straight into her eyes, held her gaze and didn't move off the dance floor. Not moving, not separating their bodies. She wanted him to kiss her. She was waiting, but he didn't. He finally loosened his grip, took her hand and they went back to the table. When they reached the table and got another drink, Donnelly, with the back of his hand, lightly brushed Tomi's thigh. Tomi didn't move. He did it a couple more times lightly down the side of her thigh. Nothing aggressive. Just a very light touch. Tomi was frozen with anticipation. *Should she reciprocate? Should she act like it's no big deal? Should she make some sort of move?* Before her brain cleared and she had the chance, he removed his hand and stopped. They spent the rest of Gemma's set sitting extremely close, Donnelly, every once in a while, touching her thigh. When a slow song came along, Donnelly had her back on the dance floor sweeping her off her feet. He was incredibly sexy and a very sensual slow dancer and knew exactly how to move. She has not been this sexually electrified since Joel. She started to have very strong guilt for feeling this way. She had to forgive herself. Joel was gone and she has a life she needed to live and not live in the painful past. She decided to give herself permission to have these feelings again.

During Gemma's break, she came over and was introduced to Donnelly. They discussed her relationship with Tomi, Agent Donnelly's career, and how Gemma made it to Nashville. All small talk but it took the sexual tension out of the air which was what Tomi needed. After Gemma's set, they decided to stay for the second band and have a couple more drinks. Donnelly helped her with swing. She wasn't great but she wasn't horrible either. She managed to keep her feet to herself. When the night ended, they both realized they had come to The Local by Uber. Donnelly offered to get them an Uber together. This way he made sure she got home safely. As they were standing outside waiting, Donnelly turned and faced Tomi. She just stared into his eyes. He was not saying or doing anything; just looking at her. She didn't know what to do. She was locked into his stare. Without saying a word, he leaned down and started to kiss her ever so lightly. She felt his warm soft lips on hers. She felt his tongue moving across her lips. She opened her lips to accept his tongue. The second she did that, his kiss got a little stronger, deeper, but still very soft. He pulled her closer and continued to kiss her until their Uber showed up. He opened the door; they both slid in and were on the way to her house.

What would she do? She doesn't know him well enough to invite him in. But that amazing kiss they just shared, she wanted more. Much more but she didn't want to seem too eager. When they pulled up to her house, Donnelly asked the Uber driver to wait. He walked her to her door, gave her an intense deep kiss, made sure she got inside safely and said, "Good Night Tomi. Go give those cajónes' a rest. I had a fun on our non-date date." He jogged down the drive to his Uber and it sped away. Tomi went inside, shut her front door and leaned against the door with her back and took a deep breath. *My God, what has come over me,* she thought. *I have not felt like this since I was with Joel.*

She cannot get the smell of Tim Donnelly out of her head. She has never smelled a man like this; and his blue eyes!

My God, I need a shower she smiled!

Chapter Twelve:
Will This Be Real?

After Tomi got home from the Local, her head was spinning with everything that happened. She took a shower, put on her pajamas and grabbed a Stella. She curled up on the couch and let the night play through her head. She went through everything over and over. But it wasn't the bombing she was thinking about. The attraction she felt for Tim Donnelly was crazy since they had literally just met. The way he dressed, the way he smelled, the way he carried himself and how he interacted with people. Outgoing, personable, funny, and welcoming. Not afraid to reach out and make friends with anybody. His intense smoldering stare with those blue eyes. His strong hands, the way he spoke very quietly and with intention directly to her while dancing with him. His strong arms around her, holding her in an iron embrace as they moved around the dance floor. She had felt then that the safest place on earth, no, the safest place in the universe, was there in his arms. They were not saying anything, just moving to the music. She goes back to the memory of him kissing her. She was hoping he would but not expecting it. When he did, he was so strong and gentle. Softly kissing at first then becoming more intense. He knew she welcomed the kiss by her reaction. He didn't let it go to waste. He was going to kiss her as long as she let him. Tomi didn't want him to stop. Her mind started to wonder what it would be like making love to him.

Her fantasy started to take shape. They were dancing in the living room. Lights down, swaying to the music. He lifted her head and started kissing her. She responded strongly. He removed her shirt and also removed his showing his strong masculine chest. Tim unhooked her bra and she let it drop to the floor. She took off her jeans. He carefully pushed her against the wall. He had both of her hands in one of his and was holding them above her head. His body pressed up against hers so she couldn't move. He took his other hand and lightly strokes her breasts. Arousing her nipples so intensely that it caused the sensation directly to her clitoris. She tried to move but didn't try very hard.

His hands moved to her legs. Lightly stroking her inner thighs. He moved his fingers just inside her panties, stroking the outer lips so softly that she can barely feel it but knows what's happening. He continued to kiss her ever so gently but intensely. His hand made it way farther into her panties. He pulls them down, spreads her legs with his leg and was now lightly stroking her. She was so wet with anticipation and he knew it. He inserted his finger inside her and felt how wet it was. He slowly lowered himself and moved her legs farther

apart. He started licking her. Not her clitoris. He saved that for later. Inside her outer lips, he went from one side to the other. As he was licking her, his finger still inside her, her breath caught in her throat and she let out a low moan of ecstasy. He knew exactly what he was doing and when he knew she couldn't stand any more, he pressed his tongue against her. Moved it ever so slightly but still applied pressure. Her orgasm exploded and she cried out. He didn't move his tongue or his finger, he kept the pressure on her while she continued to orgasm moving his finger in and out. When she could stand no more and begged for mercy, he stopped licking her but kept his finger inside her. He could feel her pumping as her orgasm subsided. She could barely stand up, so he helped her to her couch, set her down so she could recover. He took off his jeans, sat on the couch and lifted Tomi onto him. Moving her slowly up and down until he comes. Strongly holding her in place while his orgasm subsided. He kissed her intensely as he looked her straight in the eyes. He said nothing, but lifted her off him and stood up. He put his shirt and jeans back on. Leaned over and kissed her one last time. He got his coat and left. As she was imagining this scenario, her own hand was between her legs, her orgasm was intense with the thought of Donnelly. She finished, completely out of breath. Then she got up and went to brush her teeth. When she got into bed, she wondered if Donnelly was thinking the same thing about her. She wished he was here so she could smell him again and he could hold her tight like when they were dancing. *My God* she thinks, *a real man. A masculine man.* She knew few men could make her feel this way. Joel did and he was one in a million. Now Donnelly walked in and her whole world is turned upside down. She felt as though she had been struck by lightning. As she drifted off to sleep, it was as though she could feel every nerve ending tingle at the thought of him. She longed for him to hold her again. He made her feel so safe and alive. Part of her wanted to reject him because of her continued love for Joel. *Is this wrong?* The conflict swirled in her head. She loved Joel, but she had an unquenchable ache for Donnelly that laid siege to her heart.

Chapter Thirteen:
Fear in a Box

Tomi was exhausted. It was 11:30 pm and she just got home from doing a live shot on the 10:00 pm news. She had been on the bombing of Judge Moran, leading the coverage for three weeks, working on the story was all encompassing. Tomi wanted to earn her spurs on this one and prove to everyone she could dance with the finest. All of Nashville was watching, upset about the bomb in the center of their city. The murder of the Judge was a huge story and the bomber had not been caught. A light fear was gripping the city and Tomi was all over the story. When she pulled into her driveway, she noticed a small package on her front porch. *Who could have left me something?* she thought. She took the package inside and set it on the coffee table. She put her purse down, took off her shoes, and went and got an ice-cold Stella. It had been a long day and this beer was exactly what she needed. The package was wrapped in gift paper and tied with a bow. It was an 8-inch by 8-inch square and about 6 inches tall. There was no card. Tomi had no idea who would send her a present. She took another swallow of her beer and opened the package.

Once she got the wrapping off and opened the lid, there was a small explosion that knocked her back on the couch. There was so much smoke that she started to choke. In shock, she could barely think straight.

What just happened? she thought. *Oh My God.* Tomi looked around. Her living room was full of smoke and there was glitter everywhere and the stench made her gag. She was angry at herself for opening a random package, she was smarter than that. She kicked the coffee table; she ran into the kitchen. Was she alright? She started looking at every part of her body to see if there were any cuts. She didn't see any blood and felt no pain. She seemed to be OK. She grabbed her cellphone and ran outside. *I need to call the police*, she thought. *No, no, I need to call Donnelly.* She had the number for the ATF Agent in Charge, so she called him up.

Donnelly picked up his phone and said, "Tim Donnelly."

Tomi said, "Mr. Donnelly, This is Tomi Bardsley."

Donnelly responded, "Hello Tomi."

Tomi continued, "Something just happened at my house."

Donnelly asked, "What exactly happened?"

Tomi explained, "I got a package, when I opened it up it exploded."

Donnelly asked concerned, "Exploded? Are you injured at all?"

Tomi said, "No, I don't think so. I can't see anything, no blood. But it scared the Hell out of me."

Donnelly asked, "Where are you now?"

Tomi replied, "I'm outside in the driveway."

Donnelly advised, "Don't go back in the house. Wait in your car or go to a neighbor's house. Keep your phone handy. I'm sending the police, paramedics to check you, the bomb squad and ATF agents. I am on my way as well."

Tomi rang the doorbell of the neighbor's house; they welcomed her inside. She told them what happened, and she was waiting for the police and Federal Agents to arrive. The first police cars started to arrive along with the fire department and the bomb squad vehicle. She went outside and talked to the first sergeant who arrived at the scene and told him what happened and that she was waiting next door. She also him that she had called the Special Agent in Charge at the ATF. Unmarked cars arrived, men with suits got out and went into her house, police officers, blue lights, the whole neighborhood was lit up and in disarray. Fire department paramedics checked Tomi out, she was okay, no injuries. Tomi went back into the neighbor's house looking out the window at all the activity, unsure of what was exactly going on. She was shivering a bit taking it all in. She was very shaken up. In a few minutes, her phone rang.

Donnelly said, "Tomi? This is agent Donnelly. I am in your driveway in the blue Chrysler."

Tomi responded, "OK, I'll be right out." Tomi came out and sat in Tim's car.

Donnelly said, "How are you doing?"

Tomi replied, "I am kind of shaken up but I am mad at myself for opening the package. But now that all the police and the Feds are here at least I feel safe, at the moment."

Donnelly said, "Well Tomi, you are going to be safe. The agents and the bomb squad have informed me that it is not a bomb. It's not an explosive device. It was a smoke bomb, rigged with glitter and a putrid smelling liquid. Obviously meant for you to open and scare the snot out of you but not designed to injure or kill."

Tomi asked worried, "Well, who would want to do that to me?"

Donnelly responded, "Well, you are a reporter, you are a public figure so there could be lots of reasons. There are a lot of crazies in the world. What we have to be most concerned about is, is it related to the bombing of Judge Moran."

Tomi said, "Yes, of course that was my first thought. Can you tell what's inside this thing or the mechanics of it to put the two explosions together?"

Donnelly explained, "Well, at first glance, it doesn't appear to be similar. The other device was very specific in its fusing and firing. It had a lot of heavy metal parts, a lot of explosives. It was a very fiendish device. This device today is a much simpler mechanism. It doesn't appear on the face to be related but we really won't know until we send everything to the forensics lab at ATF."

Tomi asked, "OK, what do I do in the meantime?"

Donnelly replied, "In the meantime, I am going to have an agent stationed outside your house and I am going to ask Metro police to help us cruise and watch the neighborhood, just until we can get this settled to see if this is really from the bomber."

Tomi said, "I understand."

Donnelly continued, "If we find any other evidence, hopefully we can discover who it came from. Maybe we'll find out it came from an infatuated viewer or a copycat. You may find out who it is before we do. Worse case, if we find out it is the bomber, we will have to take different precautions for your safety."

Tomi said relieved, "OK, Well thank you, I really appreciate you guys getting here so quickly."

Donnelly said, "Alright Tomi. Do you think you could stay with someone tonight; do you have a friend nearby that would take you in so you can be safe and get some sleep?"

Tomi responded, "Yes, my friend Gemma, lives a few blocks away. I will call her and let her know what has happened. I can spend the night with her."

Donnelly said, "OK, well, I'm going to leave an agent here at your house and you slip to your friend's house. We will give the agent that address as well, but he'll be here at your house just in case anything suspicious happens."

Tomi said, "OK, that sounds great. Thanks Agent Donnelly."

Donnelly replied, "You can call me Tim."

Tomi said, "OK, thanks Tim. I will stay with Gemma tonight."

Donnelly responded, "Let me get Gemma's contact information so I can give it to the agent who will be watching your house and I want it as well for your safety." Tomi provided Tim with Gemma's phone number and address which was just a few blocks away.

Tomi said, "If this is the bomber, why would he target me of all the reporters covering the story? It's on every station, in every newspaper, all over the radio, it's on the web. Why would he target me? That makes me think it's not the bomber."

Donnelly said, "Well, Tomi, in watching your coverage in the last few weeks, you've done a tremendous job, but you know, some of the things you said about the bomber could have tweaked him personally."

Tomi asked confused, "What do you mean exactly?"

Donnelly replied, "Well, last week you had a report where you called him sophisticated but crazy and probably insane. One thing we never say at press conferences is whether a bomber is sophisticated or unsophisticated. If we say he is sophisticated. He will say to himself, 'I'll show you what sophisticated is' and makes the next bomb even worse, bigger, meaner, more nails, more power, more explosives. The same way if you say he is unsophisticated, that makes him madder and now he's going to show you how sophisticated he really is. We don't like to categorize them as crazy or insane or demented, as it will tweak them into lashing out. So, we try to be very circumspect what we say about bombers publicly at our news conferences. You notice how I talk about them. It's very even keeled. We are very guarded against that."

Tomi said, "OK, that makes perfect sense and I understand that. But I had an interview with a guy from the bomb squad last week and he told me that this bomber that killed Judge Moran was sophisticated and that is why I put it in my story."

Donnelly explained, "Well, the bomb squad officer is right. The bomb is sophisticated. I'm not telling you it's not sophisticated. What I'm telling you is we don't say that on television. Now, I know you are a reporter, and you got a tip from an officer on the bomb squad. Great, I know that you are going to use it. The question you had; was why would the bomber target me? My speculation is maybe he is targeting you because of some of the things you have said in your reports just like what we are discussing."

Tomi said, "OK, I totally understand it now. It was true so I was going to use that since it was an exclusive great tip."

Donnelly responded, "I understand, you got a tip, you used it. That's the way the world works. I just want you to be safe."

Tomi replied, "Thank you Tim."

Donnelly said, "Okay Tomi, we cleared the scene in your house. Go inside, pack a few things to go to Gemma's. When you're ready, come out here and get in your car. I am going to follow you to Gemma's house. I'm going to wait for you to go in to make sure you get inside. This gentleman right here, that's Agent

Monroe, he is the supervisor and he will be at your house all night and we will have another agent at Gemma's house to keep the area safe. I want you two to exchange phone numbers right now. You can call Monroe if you need to. We'll get the evidence to the lab to see if we can figure out where it came from."

Chapter Fourteen:
The Summer Wind

It had been a few days since the strange package showed up at Tomi's house. She had been an absolute fool to open it. She had not ordered anything and certainly nobody she knew was sending her anything. She had not been able to sleep. Every little sound lashed her with terror. She sat in the dark exhausted so no one could see that she was home. Now, today she got a letter slid under her door. No postage, no address, just her name. She was afraid to touch it. She moved it with her foot away from the front door and immediately called Donnelly.

Tomi said, "Tim it's Tomi."

Donnelly replied, "Hey Tomi."

Tomi said, "There has been an envelope slid under my front door."

Donnelly asked, "Did you touch it?"

Tomi replied, "No"

Donnelly expressed, "Good, I am on my way."

Donnelly raced to Tomi's house. As he drove, he thought, *this bomber is obsessed with terrifying Tomi. He was going to be a difficult and active one and I need to stay ahead of the bomber at every turn.* Donnelly arrived within 15 minutes. As Tomi opened the door, immediately she saw Tim Donnelly, and broke down. She could no longer hold herself up. She wrapped her arms around him. She was relieved of the ever-present stabbing of intense fear that had gripped her since the package explosion.

Donnelly helped her to the couch and set her down. He grabbed a blanket, covered her up and tried to calm her.

"Where's the letter?" Donnelly asked.

Tomi replied, "It's behind the door on the floor." Donnelly removed two surgical gloves from his jacket pocket, bent down and picked up the letter. As Tomi watched from the couch, Donnelly opened the envelope and read the letter silently.

Tomi asked inquisitively, "Who is it from?"

Tim replied, "It's a threat and it's from the bomber."

Tomi requested, "Tell me what it says."

Donnelly started reading, "How did you like my gift Ms. Bardsley? A person who is really insane wouldn't be able to pull that off. Wouldn't you agree? Be careful what you say about me. I can reach out and touch you just like AT&T. I noticed the cops got there awful quick. I wouldn't put too much faith in them. If they were so good, they would have me in jail by now. You need another profession. A nurse perhaps? Watch your back!"

Donnelly called one of his ATF squad supervisors to send a Special Agent right away to collect the letter. He ordered the supervisors to get the letter to the ATF lab first thing in the morning to have it processed for evidence.

Donnelly said, "Tell the lab I want fingerprints, DNA, hand writing and paper & ink analysis and I will call the Chief of Forensics lab tomorrow and have it expedited."

Donnelly sat on the couch next to Tomi. He did not say anything, he just held her as tight as he could to make her feel safe. She melted into his arms and her crying subsided. She was exhausted. Being held so tight by Tim Donnelly, she had never felt safer. She almost instantly fell asleep. Donnelly wasn't bold enough to wake her or even move. He sat quietly waiting for the Special Agent to arrive. Fifteen minutes later, Special Agent Fuller got to Tomi's house. He and his partner burst through the front door. He saw Donnelly sitting on the couch but didn't see Tomi. Fuller shouted, in a high tone "Hey Boss, the supervisor sent me for the evidence."

Donnelly glared at Fuller, "Can you be a little quieter. Ms. Bardsley is sleeping. She is scared to death so if you could keep it down that would be great."

Fuller responded, "Oh sorry boss, my bad."

As Special Agent Fuller got to work handling the envelope, Donnelly carefully inched his way out from under Tomi. She did not move. He quietly picked her up, took her to her bedroom and tucked her in. He could not stay with her, but he ordered Fuller's partner to stay behind, watch the house and keep an eye out for anything suspicious.

Two attacks on Tomi within a week. He had to make sure she was no longer in danger. He was going to see her boss, Lee Thompson, and let him know he was taking Tomi out of town and away from Nashville for a few days. She needed to be safe, and he was going to make sure that she was. Two hours later, Tim Donnelly was back at Tomi's house. The agent he left behind said everything had been quiet, he hadn't noticed anything suspicious, and Tomi hadn't moved from where Donnelly left her. The agent was relieved and Donnelly stayed behind. He wanted to get Tomi out of town but did not have the heart to wake her up. In any event, thirty minutes later, Tomi was awake. She had no idea what time it was or how she got to bed. She heard some quiet noises from her living room and slowly walked out of her bedroom and saw Donnelly having coffee.

Donnelly said to her, "Hi, looks like you finally got some sleep. I hope you don't mind I made some coffee. Do you want some?" Tomi replied, "What I could use is a drink. There is whiskey in the cupboard." Donnelly looked at her surprised. She never struck him as a Whiskey kind of girl. "I mostly keep it for guests but I can knock 'em back if I have to."

Donnelly said, "Whiskey? You're a tough cookie." He found the whiskey in the cupboard and poured Tomi a shot. He could tell she didn't drink much whiskey by the look on her face but she downed it in one swallow. Tomi grimacing, "What time is it?" Donnelly responded, "6:00 pm. You have been sleeping for a good four hours."

Tomi asked surprised, "How did I get into bed? I don't remember anything after you got here."

Donnelly replied, "You fell asleep pretty hard. After Agent Fuller got here, I put you in bed and left an agent here to make sure you were safe and to keep an eye out. I went and talked to your boss. I told him you were not safe here and needed to be kept in hiding for a few days. He absolutely agreed. What I need you to do is to pack a bag for several days."

Tomi said in an attempt to disagree, "I have a job to do, I can't leave." Donnelly stopped her mid-sentence and held up his hand.

Donnelly said, "Lee agreed with me you have to get out of Nashville. Until the bomber is identified or caught, I cannot and will not take a chance on you getting hurt or even killed. This is not up for negotiation."

Tomi asked, this time more relaxed, "Where do you plan on me going?"

Donnelly replied, "I have a safe house. I am taking you there. I'll be with you, and you'll be safe there. Besides, I have several agents in the area that will be watching the house as well."

Tomi asked, more interested, "When are we leaving?"

Donnelly replied, "As soon as you get packed. We can go shopping when we get there if there is anything you need. I want to get you out of town immediately."

Tomi crossed her arms and stood there. She watched Donnelly for a couple of minutes. His face nor his mind had changed.

Tomi shrugged, uncrossed her arms and said, "I'll go pack."

As she went to pack, she thought, *this man is a rock. He is going to keep me safe.* They were on the road within the hour. They had an eight-hour drive ahead of them. Donnelly made a fresh pot of coffee, filled a thermos and they were out the door. Donnelly decided to have an agent stay at Tomi's house. At least for the next 48 hours to watch for anything suspicious.

Little did they know, the bomber was watching from down the street. He had been there all day watching with a pair of binoculars. He saw everything. He knew he had scared Tomi Bardsley and it thrilled him; he thrived on the fear of others. He watched the comings and goings of all the agents. Now, Donnelly had returned and the bomber surmised that the agent was probably going to spend the night. The bomber decided he had better get out of there before he was seen. With Donnelly back, there wasn't anything he could do. He quietly got into his truck and headed home. If he had stayed five more minutes, he would have seen Agent Donnelly and Tomi Bardsley leave her place with a suitcase. He left planning his next move for Tomi Bardsley, unfortunately for him she wasn't going to be around. He had made a mistake.

It didn't take Tomi long to fall asleep on their trip. Donnelly had grabbed a blanket before they left and made sure she was wrapped up tight. He told her to lean her seat back, relax and just sleep, which exactly what she did. The weather was still nice and the sun was still up, so the first part of the trip had been pleasant. After a few hours, Tomi had woken up.

She was starving and wondered if Donnelly had any snacks. Of course, they didn't because they left in such a hurry. He noticed she was awake.

Donnelly said, "Well, hello there, Little One. You slept well. At least I think you did. I could tell by your snoring."

Tomi responded in a disappointing tone, "I do NOT snore. Period."

Donnelly insisted, "You sure about that, because I know what snoring is and you were definitely snoring."

Tomi said, "Well, that's my story and I'm sticking to it." They both laughed.

She had been so tired that she probably snored like a drunken sailor.

Tomi said with a little worry in her tone, "I am starving. I know it's late but could we stop and get something to eat?"

Donnelly replied, "Yes, we can. The only place really would be a gas station/minimart. I have to stop and get gas anyway." Tomi quizzed, "Gas station food?" as she tried not to make a face.

Donnelly said, "This isn't just any gas station. This is Buc-ee's." Tomi laughed. Tim said, "Buc-ee is a beaver! You'll see. They brag about the cleanest bathrooms around. I've stopped there several times and this place is pretty awesome. Do you think that I would take you to just any old gas station?"

Tomi said in a calm tone, "If you say so." She laughed and now starting to feel relaxed.

It was perfect timing. They had just finished talking and Donnelly pulled into the gas station. This thing was huge. Tomi had never seen so many gas pumps. Donnelly told her they had 60 gas pumps and could fuel 120 vehicles at once and no semi's allowed. The store was massive. She believed it had everything and anything a person needed. When she went into the bathroom, she noticed that Donnelly was right. This is the biggest, nicest, cleanest bathroom she had ever seen at a gas station. As she was coming out of the bathroom, she saw some clothing. Donnelly spotted her. He came over and Tomi said, "I'm a little chilly, I wonder if they have any long-sleeved shirts?"

Donnelly said, "I bet they do, let's go have a look." It didn't take long for Tomi to find what she was looking for. They went and got some sandwiches, chips, cheese and crackers, water, fizzy waters, a couple candy bars and they were on the road again. "That place is awesome," said Tomi. "I never thought I would say that about a Gas Station." Tim told Tomi that there is a real-life lesson to be learned from Buc-ee's. The owners, two cool Texas guys just looked at things differently. As businessmen, they looked and saw the problems travelers had on the road. Dimly lit, unsafe and dirty filling stations where no one really wanted to stop. Poor food as well and yet they knew people still needed gas and wanted safe and clean restrooms, and some decent food along with good service. They modeled their business after truck stops but for passenger vehicles and no big trucks were allowed. They found what people wanted, needed, and desired and they delivered it. Smart all the way around. All of us can use that same method of thinking used by these brilliant Texas businessmen to enhance all of our endeavors. Take note Tomi, Buccee's is an all-American success story.

Now that they were alone in the car for another 4 hours, she had better figure out how to have a conversation with Tim and hide the sexual tension that has built up. He has made her laugh, he made her relax, and he made her feel safe.

Tomi asked, "Can I still call you Tim or would you prefer Special Agent in Charge Donnelly?"

Donnelly grinned at her, "You can call me Special Agent in Charge, Mr. Donnelly Sir, Esquire, Emeritus. Should I continue to call you Ms. Bardsley or will Tomi be sufficient?"

Tomi replied cheerfully, "You can call me Her Royal Highness, Queen of the Newsroom, Lady of Breaking stories, her Lordship on High, Ms. Bardsley or Little One, I liked that." Donnelly smiled at her and they both laughed.

Donnelly said, "O.K. Tomi. Tell me a little bit about yourself. We became acquainted professionally, but I would like to know Tomi Bardsley. Not reporter Bardsley but Tomi."

Tomi warned, "That is going to be a pretty boring story. Since you are driving, I don't want to put you to sleep."

Donnelly insisted, "I disagree with that. You certainly would have had to make some life changes and career changes to be in Nashville. You told me Nashville was for a change of scenery. What was wrong with your previous scenery?" Tomi's mind instantly went to Joel. A lot of great and also sad memories came flooding back. She struggled to keep the tears in. It didn't work, as a few got away from her. Donnelly noticed the tears.

Donnelly said with so much concern in his tone, "Look Tomi, I am sorry. I don't mean to pry and of course it's none of my business. Just trying to get to know you better." Tomi knew he was just being kind and he would have no idea about Joel. Trying to keep her composure she started with Hamilton, NY. Her family, Gemma, New Jersey. Donnelly would stop her once in a while and ask a question or two. But other than that, he let her talk. He was very good at getting people to relax. All he wanted was to get Tomi's mind off of what was going on in Nashville. For the next couple of hours, he listened to Tomi Bardsley's life story. Some parts were very sad. They would make a clown cry. Some parts were excruciatingly painful. He wanted to pull over, wrap his arms around her and just hold her. She has been through a lot. Clearly, she could take care of herself. She's had to. When you're not given a choice, you don't have a choice. She felt so safe and protected when with Donnelly and now he made her laugh and relax. She found him ruggedly handsome, very masculine, and incredibly sexy.

However, Since Joel's death she was floating in a sea of doubt, reluctant to let any man close because she was ripe to be cut and hurt. When she finished talking, she was ready to learn more about Tim. He intrigued her. The appearance of Donnelly was like a splash of ice water. Maybe, just maybe she could fall in love again.

It was 2:00 am when they finally got to the hideout. To Tomi's surprise it was a beach house. She was impressed at how beautiful it was. She was expecting a sterile ATF government building, void of life and color. But this appeared to be just the opposite. She would have to wait until the morning to get a full view of the place. Donnelly grabbed her bag and led her into the house. The master bedroom was right inside the door. Tim went straight into the master bedroom. Tomi was very apprehensive as to what to do. Tim came back out of the bedroom still carrying Tomi's bag. He kept it down and asked her if she would like a drink. She said yes. Tim always made sure his refrigerator was well stocked. He was able to get an agent to go to the store and get the things he needed and wanted for this trip.

Tim got a Murphy's stout and handed Tomi a Stella. They sat on the couch. When he sat down so close to her, her breath was caught in her throat. She could feel the intensity clear down to her socks. Tim felt it too but he didn't move. They enjoyed their beers without speaking. Tomi laid her head on his shoulder. Tim put his arm around her and when he did, her sense of feeling safe had come alive. She truly felt safe and secure when nestled in his arms and she never wanted to move. When they were halfway done with their drinks, Tim took her bottle, and placed it on the coffee table next to his. He leaned over and started to kiss her. Very lightly, very sensually. So soft you could barely feel it. Tomi's stomach jumped to her throat and her nipples were instantly hard with desire. That desire exploded with colossal reverberation. But she had to maintain. She does not know this man that well and didn't want to get caught up in something that could break her. She kissed him back and when she did, his kisses got stronger and deeper. Tim held her tighter. Their kissing became so intense that it had the air of going through fire. Tim reached up and caressed her breast. He felt how hard her nipple was and his erection was so hard and strong that he struggled to hold in his desire for her. He wanted to tear her clothes off and throw her on the floor. But he knew women don't like men who can't control themselves. But they do want a man that they can arouse and would still be able to temper his sexual desire. She wanted him to take charge and to dominate but the pace and the place had to be just right. Tomi didn't move his hand. She let him massage her nipple. Man, he was good. He knew exactly when to touch, when to lightly caress and when to stop. All to drive her crazy and he was succeeding. Tomi thought she was going to have an orgasm right there on the couch. But Tim slowly stopped. He looked her straight in the eye and said, "Time for Bed." *What should she do? Does she have to follow his lead? She wanted to make love to him so badly yet she was visited by fear.* She wondered, *should she let him in entirely?* He got up from the couch, then he took her hand. She stood up. He walked over to grab her bag, he didn't go to the master bedroom, he took her upstairs and put her in one of the guest rooms. He put her bag on the end of the bed, showed her where the bathroom was. He told her that there were towels under the sink if she would like to take a shower. Before he left, he kissed her deeply and closed the bedroom door. Tomi had no words. She didn't know what to think at this moment of intense sexual tension. But what she did know for sure was that Tim Donnelly was a gentleman, pure and simple. She decided to take a shower and then noticed that the shower has a hand-held shower head. So, she stripped down and got in the shower. She was so horny that before she could even wash her hair, she put the shower head between her legs. She positioned it perfectly and allowed the pulsing water bring her to orgasm. It didn't take long and her orgasm was electric and inner burning and finished with a jolt of emotion. She was now ablaze with a desire for Tim Donnelly. She finished her shower, got into her pajamas and crawled into bed. It was 3:00 am and she was exhausted. She knew she was going to sleep like a baby knowing Tim Donnelly was downstairs. She would rather be sleeping in his arms and wondered if that would ever happen.

When Donnelly closed the bedroom door, he could barely stand up. His erection was so intense that he was afraid he was going to explode right there at the top of the stairs. He made his way downstairs, turned off all the lights and heads to bed. Like Tomi, he was wanting her in his arms right now. If nothing else, but to make her feel safe. When he sat on the end of the bed, his erection had not subsided. His mind went to the thought of kissing Tomi and caressing her nipples, she was so sexy and had this magical vibe about her. He could not stop thinking about her, she bedeviled him. He crawled into bed and fell asleep almost instantly. Still thinking about Tomi.

When Tomi woke up, she could hear rustling downstairs. She could smell coffee and bacon. She was starving. She washed her face and brushed her teeth. As she was coming down the stairs Tim looked at her and said, "Good Morning Tomi, how did you sleep?" He walked over to her, leaned down and kissed her good morning. He handed her a cup of coffee and led her to the kitchen table.

Tomi said, "I slept great. Hopefully you didn't hear me snoring from upstairs." Tim smiled and winked at her.

Donnelly responded, "Would you like any cream or sugar?"

Tomi answered, "A little cream would be nice."

Donnelly said, "You got it. I got up early to get the coffee made. I had one of my agents go to the store yesterday and get some supplies." He handed her a plate with some scrambled eggs, bacon, and a piece of toast. "Sorry about the scrambled eggs. That is all I know how to make."

Tomi smiled at him and said, "I'm sure they will be great." It wouldn't matter if they weren't. The fact that he made sure hot coffee and breakfast was ready for her when she got up, was so heartwarming. Tomi knew at that moment she was falling in love with Tim Donnelly. But was he falling in love with her?

Donnelly feeling all excited said, "When you are finished with breakfast, I would like you to go get dressed. I want to take you around town and show you the surroundings. A little later, we can go for a walk on the beach. That will clear both our heads."

Tim and Tomi headed out for a drive around town. Tim showed her the best places to eat, to people watch, to dance, and to simply just veg. They both realized that they were massive people watchers and the beach would be the perfect place. Tomi realized she had no beach attire, but it was not a problem. Tim took her to a few beach stores so she could stock up on what she needed. She bought a bikini and a cover-up but didn't let Donnelly see it when she tried it on. That is for another time. She also got shorts, beach shoes, sunglasses, sunscreen, and tank-tops. She should be set for a few days. Tim insisted on paying for her things since it was his idea to get her out of town and bring her here. They went back to the house, changed their clothes and headed to the beach. It was stunning Tomi thought. Tomi had never been to the gulf. She could not take her eyes off the water. So blue, so calm, and so inviting. She could see why people wanted to be here. You can get lost in its calmness. They grabbed their chairs, towels, radio, cooler with drinks, and headed to the water. Once they were set up, Tim said, "Let's go for a walk." As they headed out, they didn't have to say anything. Tim took hold of Tomi's hand, squeezed it lightly to let her know she was safe. The peaceful environment was wholly comforting. Having Tim next to her dulled the edge of her deep anxiety. She has not felt this way in a few years. Not since Joel. She was slowly getting over the guilt of moving on from him. Her love for him would never die but she knew she could love someone else just as much and that someone might be Tim Donnelly. Donnelly didn't show his hand and she had no idea how he felt about her. Of course, their sexual attraction was out of bounds, but does he care about her as a woman? Does he want to love her like she loves him?

They walked for about 45 minutes, turned around and headed back to their chairs. When they got there, they just sat and enjoyed the music, the sun, and the drinks. Suddenly, Mel Carter's "Hold Me, Thrill Me, Kiss Me" came on the radio. Tomi's mind went back to The Local where they danced to this song. Without saying anything, Tim took her hand, pulled her out of her chair and danced with her right there on the beach. Barely moving, holding her tight. He strokes her hair, and lightly held her head to his chest. When the song was done, Tomi looked up at Tim and they kissed. A soft passionate longing kiss. Not caring if anyone was watching. Not noticing if anyone was around. It's just Tim and Tomi on the beach. No one else. Tomi didn't want it to end. Their kiss seemed to last forever and a day. Tim knew exactly how to kiss her to stir every single nerve ending in her body. Tomi pressed her breasts against his chest. Tim's breath was caught in his throat, and he held her tighter. It was a long time before they separated. It was getting late, and they should be getting back. Once back at the house, they showered, changed their clothes and headed out to dinner. Tim knew of a great place for some amazing, blackened fish and great margaritas. They headed out to a great local place called The Costal. It was right on the water. Completely open. You can grab a table and watch the water. You can sit at the bar. If it's a little misty you can sit under the covered portion. The place was huge. The bar had two sides. The people were in various forms of dress. The place is very family friendly. They decided to just sit at the bar. Donnelly ordered a burger and a Guinness. Tomi got the grouper tacos and a Stella. The place was busy. The bartenders were very friendly and the service was great. As they drank their beers and talked about the day and what was going on in Tennessee, they got in a lot of people watching. When their food arrived, Tomi didn't realize how hungry she actually was. She tried to be dainty with her eating but she couldn't help it. She devoured her dinner. When they were finishing up, Donnelly's phone rang. He looked at it and said to Tomi, "I have to take this, I am going to step outside." It wasn't long before he returned.

Donnelly said, "Sorry Tomi, I have to leave right now. I have an agent in Memphis that has been shot. My agent here is Jody Simmons and she is going to watch out for you and take care of you. She is sitting outside but she will come in and hang out with you until you're ready to leave. In the meantime, I have to go. I'll be in touch." Donnelly leaned in, kissed her forehead and headed out. Before he got 10 feet away in walked a woman who Tomi could only assume was Jody Simmons. Jody introduced herself and sat in Donnelly's seat.

Jody said, "Ms. Bardsley, I'm Jody Simmons. I'll be with you full-time until you leave here. Not to worry, we are going to keep the appearance of best girlfriends vacationing and having a great time. In case anyone is looking."

Tomi replied, "Nice to meet you, Jody Simmons. Thank you so much. It's been a nerve wracking few weeks."

Jody responded, "I'm sure it has. I'll keep you busy to keep your mind off what is going on. Show you around and hopefully you will get to continue to relax." Tomi finished her Stella and they headed out. Jody asked Tomi if she was up for some live music and dancing. Tomi agreed and Jody took Tomi back to the beach house so she could change. Jody went home to change as well. An hour later, Jody was back in an

Uber. They went a few miles down the road to a place called Flora-Bama. It's a huge bar dance hall right on the Florida and Alabama border. Hence the name. This place was sprawling. There were so many different levels you could get lost pretty easily. They had a lively band downstairs. When you ventured upstairs to a different bar there was a single guy playing guitar and singing.

It didn't seem to matter where you went, there was someone playing music. They decided to go downstairs where the rock and roll band was playing. They each got a drink and after a while Tomi started to relax and the vibe to start dancing took over. Tomi loved music and loved to dance. She was getting better at it. When any song started, she would automatically start dancing where she stood. Jody let her know she was not to accept a dance with anyone since they were unsure of who's who. Tomi understood and they both had a great time. It was fun to go out with a female friend and relax and not worry about anything. Tomi got back to the house about 1:30 am. Jody said good-bye but not to worry. There was always an agent watching the house. Tomi was exhausted. It was a long day but a fun day. She got up the next morning, made some coffee and had an English muffin. About 11:00 am, Jody showed up at the house ready to go to the beach. Tomi got changed and they headed out. It was a beautiful sunny day. Not a cloud in the sky. Perfect beach weather. When they got to the beach and settled in, Tomi decided to ask Jody about Donnelly.

Tomi called, "Jody?"

Jody answered, "Yes."

Tomi, "Is there anything you can tell me about Tim Donnelly, personally? Do you know him well enough to give me some information about his personal life? Of course, nothing invasive."

Jody explained, "When you work for someone as long as I have, you do learn about them. It's normal. Tim Donnelly keeps his personal life pretty close to the vest, but I can tell you he's never been married. He has no kids. He had a four-year relationship with Dawn Bennett. Her modeling career took off and she had to be in New York City. They tried long distance but it didn't pan out. Tim loves his career, and he puts his all into it to making sure everything is done properly. I'm guessing that's why he's never been married. You could say he's married to his job. But what I do know is that he cares for you. I can tell by his actions." Jody's phone rang and she answered. "It's Donnelly as we speak. Hello boss. Ok. Ok. Yes, sure. I'll get it taken care of."

Tomi asked, "What's going on?"

Jody replied, "Donnelly cannot come back here to get you. He wants me to put you on a plane tomorrow. I'll get with the airlines and get something set up. You'll fly out of Pensacola."

Tomi asked, "Is Donnelly still in Memphis?"

Jody replied, "He didn't say. But in the meantime, lets enjoy the beach and get some sun."

Tomi had a hundred things running through her mind. *Where is Tim? Is he still in Memphis? I'll have to Uber from the airport. Is someone still watching my house? Did Tim arrange for an agent to pick me up? Is an agent going to continue to watch my house when I get home?*

All these things ran through Tomi's head. *Was she going to be safe when she got home? Was the shooting in Memphis going to take Tim away from the bombing case and someone else will step in?* Now she was back to being scared. She would have to wait until she was back to Nashville to find out. She wondered why Tim hadn't called her to let her know what was going on. Jody wasn't able to get a flight out until early evening. Jody and Tomi spent the day together at the beach. Went out to lunch at Tacky Jacks. Watched all the boats come in and out. They stopped at Pete's ice cream in Orange Beach. The best ice cream she's ever had. Jody knew all the best places to go. But when you live here, it's a given. It was a very relaxing day and she needed it not knowing what was next. Jody got her to the airport and they said their good 'bye's. They had become good friends and Tomi hoped it would stay that way. The flight from Pensacola to Nashville wasn't very long. She would get in at 10:00 p.m. Tomi called her boss, Lee, and told him she was heading back to Nashville. He told her things had been quiet so far in regards to the information coming out about the bombing, so she hadn't missed that much.

When the plane landed, fortunately she didn't have to go to baggage claim. Just a small carry on was all she had. As she walked to the arrival door, she stopped and started requesting a ride from Uber. Someone tapped her shoulder and said, "Excuse me Miss, your Uber is here." She looked up and to her delight and surprise, there stood Tim Donnelly. His piercing blue eyes, that gorgeous smile just looking at her. She couldn't help but smile back. He walked up to her, wrapped his arms around her and kissed her.

Chapter Fifteen:
Wallpaper Meltdown

Tomi was excited to see him. She missed him and wanted to be in his arms again kissing him and having him hold her. Tomi started thinking about what she wanted for her life. She wanted a man who was confident but not arrogant, self-assured but not cocky, tender, and loving but not soft. *Did such a man even exist in real life?* she thought...*Maybe just in the movies.* Yet, she knew that Joel was such a man, but Joel was so rare, he was so strong and yet so gentle. If she found another man like that, it would be both scary and exhilarating. She both wanted to find one and she didn't. She hoped Tim was and that he wasn't. Life seemed easier just on her own. She had friends, her career. *Men just complicated everything* she thought. Nevertheless, desire flamed inside her for Tim, and she knew that she did not have total control of this desire, it could overwhelm her.

When Tim saw Tomi's smile at the airport his heart melted. He saw her as both the girl next door and an exotic creature. Her strength in doing her job and her vulnerability when not doing her job. She's had to be strong. Her family life had not been easy. The loss of her first love was devastating. Tim worried if he could compete with a memory. If someone was divorced or the relationship didn't work, the two people go their separate ways like him and Dawn. That was completely different. When someone loses the person, they love most and someone new comes along, it's always hard for that new person to compete with the memory. *Are you being compared to the lost love?* You are obviously sympathetic to their loss and want them to carry those wonderful memories. Hopefully, those memories will still be there but just maybe, hopefully they may fade a little bit to let the new love in. Only time would tell on that. The only thing Tim knew he could do was to love Tomi, give her time, and show her he is the man she can turn to. The man she can trust. The man she can love completely without destroying the memory of Joel. Tim hoped she would let her guard down enough to let him in. After that, he will do the rest.

Donnelly offered, 'Let's get you home and in your own bed." He called the agent watching Tomi's house. Let's them know she was coming home and ordered that an agent would continue to watch the house until all this mess was done. Donnelly got Tomi home, helped her inside, then checked out her house just to make sure everything was OK. It was late and he was sure she was happy to be home. He put her bag on her bed, took her hand and led her to the living room. He grabbed her, held her tightly, and kissed her deeply. He told her he'd missed her.

Donnelly said concerned, "You need to get some sleep. You are totally safe. Good night Little Bit and I'll talk to you tomorrow."

Tomi replied, "Thank you so much for picking me up at the airport and bringing me home."

Donnelly responded, "I wouldn't have it any other way."

Before Tomi could think about it, "Please stay the night with me," popped out of her mouth.

Donnelly asked, "Are you sure that's what you want? Because I sure do."

Tomi reassured, "It's exactly what I want." Donnelly called the agent watching the house and informed him he won't be needed any longer tonight.

An evening just to themselves now made her both excited and apprehensive. Their first night together. They can be themselves. No talk of Judge Moran or bombings. Just the two of them being together. However the evening went, she was going to embrace every moment. She wasn't going to worry about how things would go, where they were going or how the evening would end. She was going to absorb this special time she has with Tim Donnelly. She went to the refrigerator, took out a couple of beers, frozen glasses and got some cheese and crackers from the cupboard. They took off their shoes, sat on the couch let the day melt away.

Tim knew the evening was going to be perfect. He felt it to the center of his being. All he could think about was Tomi. Kissing her, holding her, dancing in the living room with her, keeping her safe, etc. Letting her know she was safe with him. She was a strong but vulnerable woman, but even strong women need to know someone is keeping them safe. His aura was different. He had this soothing effect about him that she couldn't quite place her finger on. She couldn't help but smile. Her smile was so big, it took up her whole face. Tim smiled back. He put his arms around her and kissed her so deeply that all she could do was melt into his arms. His kiss was so sensual, so soft and deep. Tim held Tomi tight. He wanted her to know she was safe. She would always be safe. When the kiss ended, Tomi went into the kitchen and pulled two glasses out of the freezer, handed one to Tim and a Murphy's. "Ah, so you remembered!" he said. "Of course, hello, that's all I've ever seen you drink. It was easy to deduce," Tomi said giggling. She pulled out the cheese and crackers, they went into the living room and sat on the couch.

She had Motown playing in the background. Four Tops, The OJay's, The Temptations, Marvin Gaye, Sam, and Dave. There was something about Motown that got Tomi moving. The minute she hears it, she starts moving, starts dancing right where she stands. Tim found it endearing. The music started and so does Tomi. Tim sat so close, it's like they were glued together. He put his arm around her, held up his glass and said, "Here's to excellent reporting." Tomi held up her glass and responded, "Here, here." Tim said, "Now, that's all we are going to say about work. This night is for us and I don't want any bombing talk to get in the way."

Tomi replied, "I totally agree."

As they sat drinking their beer, snacking on cheese and crackers, they talked about life. They talked about each other's lives. Their upbringing and their past mistakes. Some of them were hysterical. It was a magical wonderful time. There was no stress and no tension. Just a lot of laughing. In the course of their conversation, once again Mel Carter came on Pandora. Tim automatically got up, took Tomi's hand and started dancing with her. He knew "Hold Me, Thrill Me, Kiss Me" was Tomi's favorite song. He had been listening to the song over and over so he would know the words. He sang along perfectly. He sang directly to Tomi. She knew it. She knew he was talking directly to her. When the song ended, Tomi took Tim by the hand and led him down the hallway to her bedroom. She was a sexually charged woman and was not afraid of what she wanted. Right now, all she wanted was Tim. Dreaming was over, it's now time for action. He's here and he's real. When they got to the bedroom, Tim saw a very cozy room. Not overdone with pillows and stuffed animals. There was beautiful mauve and gold wallpaper. Just on one accent wall.

Huge plant in the corner. Lavender velvet chair in front of the plant. It had three rhinestone buttons on the back. Very girly but not gaudy. There was a full-length mirror nestled in another corner. She had a small salt lamp to give the room just enough lighting to make it romantic and you can surely see what you are doing. Soon enough they started kissing, as the tension was already kicking in. Tomi stopped and took off her top. She was wearing an incredibly sexy bra. Pink and cream with satin ribbons and two small pearls right in the center. Tim was blown away. He took off his shirt. His strong chest, his narrow hips, and his muscular arms sent shock waves through Tomi's body. Tomi moved forward and undid his belt, then the button and the zipper of his jeans. She slid them down along with his boxer briefs to his ankles. She had him step out. She took the lavender chair, moved it in front of the mirror and had Tim sit down. Tim did what he was told as it was clear that Tomi had something already planned. Tomi removed her bra and her shorts but left the matching thong in place. Tim could see everything. Tomi then knelt in front of him. Tim's breath caught in his throat. Tomi slowly began to fellate him. Tomi was extremely sensual, soft and gentle. She worked slowly, never in a hurry, making love like this meant something to her and she wanted Tim to feel it too. Tim's erection was so hard that he struggled to control himself. She lightly grabbed him and slowly moved her hand up and down. Very lightly, softly stroking the shaft while she had him in her mouth. He watched in the mirror. This beautiful woman on her knees between his legs, wearing nothing but a thong was a visual he could not take his eyes off. He was going to explode if he did not control himself. He made her stop. He got up and slowly walked her back against the wall. He was holding her hands above her head. *OMG* Tomi thought, just like the fantasy she had when she first met him. He asked her if she had ever been frisked. She whispers, "No". Tim told her to keep her hands above her head and do not move them. He pulled down her thong. Lightly moved her legs apart, and then knelt in front of her. He had thought about this moment for months. It was sexier and more erotic than he had ever imagined. She smelled divine. She was so sweet and soft. He put his mouth on her moving slowly from one side to the other. He put one hand between her legs and felt for the opening. She was so wet that she was dripping. This drove Tim crazy. He slowly and gently inserted his finger inside her. Tomi whimpered but did as instructed and didn't move her hands. Tomi was struggling to control herself. She wanted to wait but it was getting harder and harder. Suddenly, Tim put his tongue on her. He just put enough pressure on her and she exploded. She could no longer keep her hands above her head. She lowered them and gripped the door jamb to hold on. She was coming with such intensity that her knees buckled but she held on. Tim didn't stop. He continued with his finger and was sweetly ravaging her with his mouth. Her orgasm was strong and intense, she didn't think it would ever end. Tim still did not stop. Finally, when she could take it no more, she begged for mercy. Tim stood up, kissed her deeply, and helped her to the bed. He laid down beside her as she shuttered. She was not cold; it was the aftermath of her most unbelievable orgasm. She had been waiting for and dreaming about this for weeks and it was 1000 times better than she imagined. As she recovered and her breathing slowed, she turned to Tim. He was lying on his back. She once again put him in her mouth. His erection had not subsided at all. After a few strokes, she could taste the beginnings of him leaking out. She stopped, straddled Tim, and slowly lowered herself on to him. When she sat all the way down, he filled her completely. The sensation caused Tomi's sexual desire to stir again. Tim's mind raced. How sweet, soft and tight she was and he fills her perfectly. Tomi slowly climbed off and turned around. She sat back down on Tim but now with her back to him. She had her hands around his ankles as she moved up and down. She continued to move. Slowly and deliberately. No heavy pounding, just a rhythmic movement that was very sensual. Tomi was using Tim's body against her for the perfect amount of friction to get her going again. Tim could not take it any longer. So, he stopped Tomi, had her move off him. Told her to get on her hands and knees. He got behind her and entered her from behind. The sensation for both stopped their breath. He could no longer hold back. As he started to take Tomi, he had his hands on her hips so he could get deeper. He noticed Tomi put her hand between her legs and he could feel her hand between his. She was masturbating. What a turn on. He was taking her from behind and she was masturbating. They could see everything. They were able to watch everything. Each other's reactions, facial expressions. This had to be the most erotic thing Tim has ever experienced. That was it, Tim had to let go. Crying out in his own explosive orgasm. Tomi was able to masturbate herself into a second orgasm at the same time as Tim's. When his orgasm calmed down, he didn't pull out. He kept pumping inside Tomi. The sensation was incredible, and he didn't want it to end. Tomi didn't move as she didn't want to disturb anything Tim had going. She wanted him to feel every part of his orgasm until it subsided.

When it finally did, they both laid down exhausted, satisfied, and hungry for more. Tomi grabbed a blanket and covered them both. Tim grabbed her, pulled her close, and wrapped his arms around her. They didn't speak. They just laid there in each other's arms. Basking in their explosive orgasms. Eventually, they both fell asleep wrapped up together. Tomi didn't want it to end. This was where she wanted to be. Always.

Tim Donnelly has never been married. He has no children; he has never really been in love with anyone. His career was his main love. Can he love a woman as much as his career? Can she pull him away just enough for love and how can she make that happen? Did the end of his last relationship do damage? What she knows about Tim Donnelly reminds her of the Eagles Song "Desperado" with the last line being "You better let somebody love you, before it's too late." Is she that woman? She wants to be that woman. With previous relationships before Joel, you realize you can't change people. People have to want to change. They have to want to be in a relationship and give it 100%. There are some who refuse or simply just cannot. This caused Tomi to tread lightly. Even her own wisdom was an obstacle. A naiver woman would jump in with both feet. However, Tomi's no ingenue. Tim knew this woman was for him. He wanted this woman for himself. Does she want the same thing? he wondered. They would worry about that later. For now, they were both enjoying an incredible night that neither of them will ever forget. Tim closed his eyes and drifted off to sleep with Tomi right beside him.

Chapter Sixteen:
Scales Tip Back

Donnelly was focused. He had been on this case almost a month and he wanted to break it wide open. The murder of a Judge was something that struck at the heart of the criminal justice system. If bombers and killers could take out Judges, then there is no real justice in America and Donnelly knew how important the case was. Donnelly called a command meeting at the ATF division office in Nashville. Present were the supervisors he had working on the case from his bomb and arson group to his intelligence supervisor. He also had his ATF case agents present. He had the Metro Police Bomb Squad Lieutenant, a Lieutenant from the Metro Homicide Bureau, he had an ATF profiler in from Quantico, an FBI Supervisor and a supervisor from the ATF forensics lab in Atlanta. All there to discuss the case and the direction of their investigation efforts.

Donnelly liked to set the course, direction and speed on a big investigation and he needed everybody on board to get it done. Everybody settled into the large conference room. They knew Donnelly's style and he always listened to them all, they had deep respect for him. But today, he wanted to move things along quickly and he was going to send some orders out.

Donnelly addressed, "Good Morning Everyone. So, I brought you all in to talk about the direction of the case. To talk about some of the major lead categories and see which way we are going. We have got to get a break in this case. You know how it is. If we can't get them, we have to force them. So, let's see where we are today and see what could happen this week." Donnelly called on the squad supervisor Bill Hightower.

Donnelly said, "Bill, let's talk about all the leads we have since the last meeting. What are we moving on?"

Hightower responded, "Well, boss, we set a bunch of leads on people that the Judge had sentenced to long prison terms. We started out with the longest prison terms and planned on working our way back. It was quite a list because he had been in charge of felony criminal cases for a long time. Of course, we also started with the freshest cases. "

Donnelly asked, "How has that been going?"

Hightower replied, "Well, it's been good but it's a lot of work. We got inmates scattered throughout the state in various prisons in Tennessee that the Judge has sentenced to many years. So, we've covered about a dozen of those inmates so far. What we do is, we go and review the file then we go to the prison and interview the inmate. If any leads develop, any family members, known criminal associates, conspirators from the initial crime, former cellmates we want to talk to, we try to flush that out. We try to talk to the detective who worked the case to see if there is anything there.

If anyone was mad at the Judge or if there were any threats made previously, we are going through that process. "

Donnelly responded, "OK Great, how many do you have left?"

Hightower said, "Well, initially we just wanted to go back a few years so we have about six more left that we think were significant prison time. So, all in all we will probably have about 18 in this first section. If we don't develop anything there, we will move on to some later cases."

Donnelly expressed, "OK, that sounds good. Sounds like you are progressing. Do you need any more manpower or help?"

Hightower replied, "No, I think we can get through this first bunch pretty quickly but if we have to go through a second layer, we might need some more agents."

Donnelly said, "OK, you let me know if you need anything else and I'll get it to you. Thank you, Bill. Let's move over to the FBI Supervisor Jacob Hardcastle. "Jake, give us an update on any terrorism related leads." Jake: "Yes sir we've swept all our indices and databanks and we are not picking up any indicators of terrorism. We did a cursory review of all the Judge's cases and we did not find any evidence of him sentencing any terrorism related defendants."

Donnelly: "Ok, thanks Jake, as you all know on terrorist bombings the FBI takes the lead. On Criminal bombings the ATF takes the lead. But we always pull together as a strong team and we will keep it going that way. Let's move to the findings from the forensics lab and talk about some of the leads coming out of there so let's have the case agent detail us all on the forensics. Brenda, how about outlining for the group what you have coming out of the laboratories so far."

Brenda got ready and said, "Yes sir, well we have gotten a lot of reports back from the ATF lab so far. Of course, we all know that we found a lot of welded steel and the explosive technology branch and the laboratory have been able to piece that steel back together. Very unusual construction."

Donnelly asked, "How so? We know we had it but how is it totally configured in the bomb?"

Brenda answered, "It looks like a rectangle. Picture a rectangle made of welded steel with one side missing. We thought at first, we had a box, a complete box, but we didn't. And we believe the components of the device were all inside the welded box with the fusing and firing mechanism on the side

of the box that was closed and the explosives in the middle and then the shrapnel which included nails and ball bearings toward the open end of the box. "

Donnelly chipped in, "Yeah that looks like a consistent view from what we saw at the scene. The Judge really took a lot of those nails and ball bearings and that car was riddled with it."

Brenda affirmed, "Correct. So, it looks like it was all designed to be directional. Of course, Boss, you know we did find remnants of a Servo motor inside the blast crater and inside the Judge's car, so we all know it was triggered by remote-control or command detonation as we call it. We connected the servo parts to a particular transceiver that is used as part of a model airplane transmitter. It is kind of an unusual remote-control set. "

Donnelly asked, "You know who makes that remote-control airplane?"

Brenda answered confidently, "Yes sir, we called the manufacturer in Dubuque Iowa, we got a list of all the remote model airplanes with that particular transmitter being sent to us from Dubuque. They do ship all over the country. So, we are waiting for that list to come in."

Donnelly responded needing more information, "Alright, that's good. Can you brief us on anything about the power system?"

Brenda responded, "Well, we have some batteries identified. It looks like they are Duracell's. We are talking to the ATF guy who specializes in the batteries and we are also going to Duracell to see if we can get any kind of description from the guts we have found. We aren't sure exactly what they were, we're hoping Duracell and our battery guy can put it together for us."

Donnelly replied, "OK well, sounds like me might develop some leads out of those forensics."

Brenda added, "Oh, there is one other thing Mr. Donnelly, the lab tech had found a lot of black electrical tape. Very small pieces inside the remnants of the device."

Donnelly responded, "Oh, I remember the national response team mention that at the bomb scene."

Brenda affirmed, "Yes Sir, they also recovered some electrical blasting cap like wire fragments and we think it's Dupont and the black electrical tape so we do have some things to work on and maybe match."

Donnelly said, "Okay, thanks again Brenda. Let's move on to the Supervisor of the Forensics Lab, Lloyd McCarthy." Donnelly began, "Okay Lloyd, what can you tell us about the explosives?"

McCarthy answered, "Well, Mr. Donnelly, it's TNT. The standard grade military explosives."

Donnelly said, "Alright Lloyd, tell us how you found it."

McCarthy continued, "Residue all over the metal box, residue on the nails taken from the Judge's body. We have it everywhere at the scene."

Donnelly responded, "Well, we don't see TNT much in bombs. It's usually dynamite, black powder, gun powder, C4, etc. Brenda, can you check the Explosives Incident System Database to see if there is any stolen TNT from the Military in the last three years?"

Brenda said, "Yes Sir."

Donnelly said, "Thanks Lloyd. Now, let's move on to the profilers. As you all know we have Gus Barry in from Quantico. How are you doing Gus?"

Gus said, "Hi Boss, it's good to see you. "

Tami Ryan and Jim Cavanaugh

Donnelly said, "I don't know if you guys know but Gus and I went to the ATF academy together and we were also on the national response team together so we are old pals. "

Gus confirmed, "That's right, I know everything about the boss."

Donnelly cut Gus jokingly, "You can just shut up about that stuff Gus, I didn't bring you here for that."

Gus said laughing, "Okay boss, I'll save that for later. Just one thing, I'm sure nobody here knows that you are the only Agent that ever yelled, 'Drop the God Damn Chihuahua'."

Everybody roared and Tim just rolled his eyes at Gus.

Donnelly said, "Thanks for that Gus, now I just want to talk about following leads, OK?"

Gus responded, "Okay."

Donnelly asked, "What can you tell us? What do you think we got here? Anything you can help us with?"

Gus answered, "Well, of course, it's tough to tell from just the device but he looks like a very organized person. This bomb, from what we can tell, took a lot of time and effort to put together. All the welding work, the electrical work, the remote-control, the planning, the placement, using a directional aspect of the bomb to kill the Judge. Placing it in the stolen car next to where the Judge always parks. All this takes a lot of planning and organization and was incredibly unique."

Donnelly said, "Yes, as you guys all know the bomber put the bomb on the passenger side of a stolen car and parked it next to the Judges normal parking spot, near the coffee shop. When the Judge arrived that morning, the bomber detonated the bomb by remote-control and slung the ball bearings and nails through the Judge who was just getting out of his driver's seat. It blew him back across the front seat onto the passenger door which was hanging off the hinges. It was quite a gory scene for those of you who weren't present, and it was a very unique placement. This bomber had to steal the car, make this bomb and as Gus said, he is very organized. OK Gus, so knowing what we know about the bomb, what can you give us or suggest a way we should proceed to get ahead of this guy?"

Gus continued, "Well, sometimes guys like this are so into their case they just can't leave it alone. They are obsessed with it and there is the possibility that he was at the bomb scene that morning. One: Since he had to use his remote-control, he was nearby. Those things are line of sight and you know they only go about a half a mile. Like a garage door opener. So, we know he had to be there when the bomb detonated. That means he didn't have to race away immediately."

Donnelly said in affirmation, "Correct, we have had cases like that in the past so you think we ought to work that pretty hard?"

Gus said, "Yeah, it's just something we need to cover." Hightower speaks up.

He said, "We do normally have an agent film the crowd at all bomb scenes and we did that morning as well. I think it was Joey Jones, I had him do that so we can watch some film of the crowd that morning but it wasn't until we tasked him to do it, so it may not be everybody who was there at every moment. "

Donnelly said, "Right, so let's get Joey's film and I want all you guys here to review it and also let's get some film from the news people. We had all the channels there. They were all filming; we can request them. Let's get Fuller and get him in here and we'll get Fuller to make a request of all the news stations to get any footage of the crowd. Mostly they will cooperate because it's probably in the background of their video footage that they put out anyway. "

The next day, Donnelly gets a call from Tomi Bardsley.

Tomi said, "Hey Tim."

Donnelly replied, "Hello Tomi."

Tomi continued, "We got a request from Agent Fuller that you guys want some footage from the morning of the bombing of the Judge."

Donnelly confirmed, "Yes, that's right, we are asking all the news outlets to provide any footage they have. We just want to sweep the crowd to see if we can see anything."

Tomi said, "Well, I've got it; it was mostly my crew so I'll be glad to bring it over so you can take a look at it. But of course, if it's big news I want the exclusive!"

Donnelly said laughing, "You know Tomi, I'll always give you the exclusive."

Tomi said, "I hope so Tim."

Donnelly said, "Okay, bring it over in the morning and I'll have the crew ready to look at it and I appreciate the call, Thanks Tomi." The next morning, Tomi and her cameraman arrived. They set up a monitor in the conference room and Donnelly brought back the squad supervisor Bill Hightower, Case agent Brenda Humphrey, and three other agents in the squad along with the Intelligence Supervisor. He had the Metro Police Bomb Squad Lieutenant, and the detective sergeant from Metro Homicide. All assembled in the conference room. Tomi ran the video so everybody could get a look at the crowd to see if they can see anything that stood out. About halfway through the video, Brenda Humphrey hollered, "Stop, right there! Hold it! Look at that guy." Tomi stopped the video and backed up. Brenda got up out of her seat. Went to the screen and pointed.

Brenda continued, "That guy right there in the green shirt. I know that guy."

Donnelly ordered, "Hold it, hold it right there. How do you know that guy?"

Brenda continued, "Well, I don't know him but I have seen his picture before."

Donnelly asked, "Where?"

Brenda continued, "Well, we went to the state prison to interview this guy the other day who had been sentenced by Judge Moran."

Donnelly clarified, "Well that can't be him Brenda because he's in prison."

Brenda said in affirmation, "Yes sir, of course, I know it's not him. It's not the guy we interviewed. You see while we were interviewing him, we asked to see the visitor logs and we noticed on the visitor logs he only ever had one visitor. We asked the corrections officer about it and he told us that's the guy's brother. He's constantly here, he stays for the whole visitation. He never misses one and he never leaves. He's the only guy that ever comes. So, we asked him more about him. The corrections officer says 'I'll pull the file.' The Corrections Officer told us that whenever a visitor comes in to visit a lifer, we always do a workup sheet so we know whose coming in. We went to the corrections officer's office; they pulled the file on this guy's brother and that's him! That's him right there standing in the green shirt. That's the guy's brother."

Donnelly sought more information, "So what you are telling me is the guy doing life sentenced by Judge Moran, his brother was at the bomb scene?"

Brenda confirmed, "That's right, That's him. We saw his driver's license photograph that was in the file that the corrections officer had."

Donnelly said, "Okay Well, what about the case about the guy in prison. What's the story on that?"

Brenda replied, "I don't know, it's pretty basic. He killed his wife; he was convicted of it and Judge Moran sentenced him to life. It looks like a straight domestic murder." Donnelly turned to the sergeant of homicide and asked, "sergeant do you remember the case?"

The sergeant replied, "Oh, I remember the case; I didn't work it but we have some of the detectives in homicide that did. I'll get the files and take a look at them to see if there is anything else in there of interest."

Donnelly said, "OK, Great. Thanks sergeant. Brenda, this is important, I want you to find out more about this guy. The brother. Where he lives, what he's about, see if you can come up with something. Research the case with homicide. This might be a lead. Remember if the guy lives in Nashville he could have come out to the scene of the bombing just out of curiosity like hundreds of other people do. So, let's not get our hopes up too big because it's a lead but it does have a little bit of promise. You all work on this, this afternoon and we will meet again tomorrow afternoon to see what you can dig up and set our new course of direction and speed."

Don't stop on anything else. Let's press on all fronts until we can force a break.

The next afternoon, investigators assembled again and Donnelly asked Brenda to start the briefing.

Brenda responded, "Yes sir, Well the inmate we interviewed was Lonnie Miller, he was a resident of the Hermitage neighborhood of Nashville who was convicted of killing his wife three years ago. It was a very brutal case. So, when we went to the prison and discovered his only visitor was his brother and was confirmed by the picture we saw yesterday. His brother's name is Sparky Miller. He lives in South Pittsburg in East Tennessee. We know he's a welder, served in the Navy."

Donnelly asked surprised, "He's a welder!?"

Brenda confirmed, "Yeah, that stuck out at us too, boss, because of the welded box."

Donnelly said, "Yes, okay, but there are a lot of welders around. Go ahead."

Brenda continued, "Well, he was an electrician in the Navy."

Donnelly replied, "Interesting."

Brenda expressed confidently, "Yes sir, but now he lives in South Pittsburgh and we have done some interviews over there trying to find out if anybody knew him. We talked to the sheriff, we talked to the detectives. He's known around there but all he has is a minor criminal record. Drunk and disorderly years ago. He's not some sort of active criminal."

Donnelly said, "Okay. Thanks Brenda. Sergeant, what do you have on the homicide of Lonnie Miller's wife? What can you tell us about that?"

The sergeant began, "Yes, Mr. Donnelly, I have the file right here. The detective that worked the case couldn't make it, he's in court today but if you need to talk directly to him, I can arrange that. Jo-Sue was 36 years old. She was a part-time bank teller at bank in Donelson. She seemed to have no enemies that we could find. There didn't seem to be a reason for anyone else to kill her and so the detectives centered on her husband. It was a particularly brutal case though and that is the thing the detective pointed out to me when I asked him about it, he said 'I don't think I can ever forget that case'."

Donnelly said wanting to know more, "Interesting, so what happened?"

The sergeant continued, "She was pretty clean. No reason for anyone to want to kill her. But she did have a lot of conflict with her husband Lonnie."

Donnelly asked, "What kind of conflict?"

The sergeant responded, "Well, the Hermitage precinct had been called to their address on several occasions in the past few years for reports of domestics. Neither party was ever arrested for anything. There was just a lot of strife in the marriage. That was in the file, relatives said they fought a lot. Jo-Sue was very controlling. Lonnie was dominated by her. It was an unusual marriage for sure. He was also having an affair with a woman named Delores who lived three blocks away."

Donnelly said, "Okay, understood. There are a lot of marriages like that, that don't end up with murder."

The sergeant said, "Yeah, you got that right boss. But the way this woman was murdered, it's unbelievable."

Donnelly quizzed, "Okay, why don't you tell us what happened?"

The sergeant said, "Well, they found her in the basement, she was naked, she was hog-tied with her hands behind her back. Feet bent up behind her buttocks and tied to her hands."

Donnelly sought for more details, "Wow, that is a pretty powerless position. Was she alive when she was bound like that?"

The sergeant replied, "According to the coroner she was. She struggled to get out of the bindings. There was a lot of marks on her hands and ankles which proved she was moving and straining significantly to get free."

Donnelly asked, "How was she murdered exactly?"

The sergeant explained, "Well, it looks like the killer stood over her. Maybe straddled her, and put a ligature around her neck, a big loop and he would hold the other side of the loop. He would pull up on the ligature that was around her neck which would put the weight of her body on her throat. This would cause her to expire."

Donnelly said in a low tone, "Well, that is pretty unusual."

The sergeant continued, "Yes well, there is more. The coroner said there were multiple marks and many locations on her neck. That means the killer repeatedly lifted her up chocking her, almost killing her and then releasing the ligature. It was torture. He was torturing her. He'd lift her up and let her back down over and over. With the position she was in, she was powerless to keep the weight of her body off her throat.

She was almost killed a dozen times before she finally died, according to the coroner. "

Donnelly said, "Okay, that is some pretty brutal stuff. Gus, what do you think about that?"

Gus responded, "We have seen a lot of murders like that but that method is usually from some brutal serial killers. But one thing I would ask is, was she sexually assaulted?"

The sergeant replied, "No, there were no signs of sexual assault. Just the ligature and the torture, oh, and a bloody nose. She was struck a few times." Gus chipped in, "I think she was naked and tied like that for two reasons, one to humiliate her and two, to torture her. The killer is getting a humiliation factor here. The killer really, really hates this woman or he's a depraved serial killer."

Donnelly asked, "Was the basement locked? Was there any evidence of forced entry?"

The sergeant answered, "According to the reports there was no forced entry and that is why they centered so much on the husband. Plus, the victim scrawled his initials on the countertop in blood. He had a motive as he was having an affair and he also made incriminating statements wishing she was dead. So, no forced entry, no enemies, no reason for anyone else to kill her. The place was all locked up. They charged the husband, he got convicted. There are a couple of other interesting facts."

Donnelly asked, "What is that, sergeant?"

The sergeant replied, "Well, the ligature Lonnie used to choke her was never found. Her clothes were missing. The detectives figured he took them and hid them somewhere or threw them away to conceal any evidence. He had gone on a fishing trip the next day and detectives think he may have thrown that stuff in the lake in Alabama."

Donnelly quizzed, "Well he left her hog-tied right?" The sergeant said, "Yes, he left her hog-tied but the ligature he used around her neck was different. It was a loop. When he decided to kill her, he just pulled up on the loop and held her head up until she was dead. For some reason, Lonnie took the loop off of her head and her clothes have never been found."

Donnelly said, "Okay, interesting. Thanks sergeant. Thanks Gus. Anything else you want to add Gus?"

Gus responded, "No, I think you got it all. You are dealing with one depraved and violent killer with Mrs. Miller, but I don't see why or how it's going to connect to the bomber since you already have the killer of Mrs. Miller."

Donnelly said, "Correct, and now we have the brother to look at so we will see what happens."

In a couple of days Bill Hightower called Donnelly and said, "Hey Boss, Brenda is over in East Tennessee, and she wants to talk to you. She is on the phone. Can we come to your office?"

Donnelly answered and said, "Yes come on down." Hightower went downstairs to Donnelly's office, and they got Brenda on the speaker phone.

Donnelly said, "Hi Brenda."

Brenda replied, "Hey Boss, I got a lead I want to talk to you about and what we found."

Donnelly was eager to hear what it was, "Great, go ahead."

Brenda began, "We got the list back from the model airplane company in Dubuque for where all the exact model of the remote-control transceiver were shipped anywhere in the southeast. We first started with the leads in Tennessee and then planned to later go to Kentucky, Alabama and Georgia just to branch out. Then we broke the lead on the brother of Lonnie Miller so we are over in South Pittsburgh. While we were here, we checked against the list of the model airplanes the company had sent us. They sent a number of these units to a Hobby Lobby in Chattanooga. So, I sent some agents over to the Hobby Lobby in Chattanooga to pull the receipts for any of that particular model remote-control transceiver. They had a cash sale about a month before the bombing and we pulled their video tapes from the security camera and buying one of these remote-control transceivers and model airplanes was Sparky Miller."

Donnelly said, "OK, Wow. Great break in the case Brenda, Good work!"

Brenda said with a warm smile, "Yes Sir."

Donnelly added, "Alright, so look, we know his brother was sentenced by Judge Moran, we know he lives in East Tennessee, we know he's a welder, we know he's an electrician and now you have video of him buying the exact model airplane transceiver a month before the bombing and we know he was present at the bomb scene immediately after the bombing because we have him in the video we got from Tomi Bardsley. That's enough, Brenda, to get us a federal search warrant for Sparky Miller's house in South Pittsburgh. I want you to draw up the affidavit today and we'll plan on searching in the morning."

Brenda: "We'll get right on it."

Donnelly continued, "Bill, get a team assembled to do the search. This guy looks pretty wild, we might want to bring in the Special Response Team to serve the warrant and we will probably need more agents. Certified Explosives Specialists and some Explosive Technology Branch and Explosives officers to help us do the search. A bomber like this could have boobytraps everywhere.

Hightower responded, "Yes sir, I'll get on the phone right away and we will get them all here. When do you want to do the warrant?"

Donnelly replied, "Well, let's get it signed today, assemble our team tomorrow and we will do it first thing in the morning the day after tomorrow."

Hightower said, "Yes sir."

Donnelly concluded, "Okay. Thank you."

Chapter Seventeen:
Machinations of the Law

Donnelly assembled his commanders to prepare for the search warrant execution on Sparky Miller's house in South Pittsburg, East Tennessee. Donnelly had earlier set a surveillance team on the house to see if Miller was actively coming and going from the residence. So far, they had reported no activity. Nevertheless, he was prepared for what they might face. Bombers were the ATF's business, and they knew how to deal with them. He also called in a Special Response Team or SRT. ATF called their Swat teams SRT. But in essence it is the exact same function. A tactical team made up of supervisors, leaders, tactical operators, negotiators, medics, dog handlers, long rifle teams sometimes called snipers, were all part of the team. They can deploy gas, they can shoot a long shot, they can breach doors, they can get into inaccessible places. They also use flash bangs and special cameras to be able to deal with violent and dangerous subjects of all kinds. Just about everyone ATF deals with is somehow involved in guns, bombs, arson, and many are people who are violent or capable of violence.

Donnelly stood to address everyone, "OK, everyone, we are ready to hit the house of the suspect in the killing of Judge Moran. You've all been briefed on the details. We've had the residence under surveillance, we've noticed no activity there. It's a small frame home. Looks to be about 1500 square feet.

"Miller's a Navy veteran with only a minor criminal record from a long time ago. He is a welder and was an electrician in the Navy, so he has those skills. We suspect he made the bomb that killed Judge Moran and this is a search warrant to find the evidence and hopefully his bomb factory. Let's hear from the tactical supervisor now."

The Tactical Supervisor of the Special Response Team, laid out his diagram on the conference table showing Miller's residence and the surrounding area.

The Tactical Supervisor said, "The Surveillance has shown nothing in the last day or so boss, no activity there but we are very cautious that he still could be laying low if he thinks the police are on to him. Also, that he may have booby-trapped the premises. Our plan is to make a slow entry since we see no activity. Get up to the door, do a breach and hold and of course announce our authority and purpose. If we find no activity, we'll move in slowly because of the danger of booby-traps and bombs. Once we can safely clear the residence, we will bring in Explosives Enforcement Officers from the Explosive Technology Branch and Certified Explosives Special Agents to make sure that the place is devoid of any booby-traps or other devices." If we encounter Miller, of course we will have negotiators there and they have his background and they are prepared to try to make him surrender peacefully. His house is small, the property is not to awfully large. We've gone over it pretty well. We feel like we will have it all secured pretty quickly and we are ready for any contingency. We are ready to move on your word Mr. Donnelly."

Donnelly said, "Okay, Lou thanks. Let's set the operation for first light, 6:00 a.m. in the morning. We'll move in then. If we can get Miller detained that is great, if not, I want a thorough search of the premises. I want to know if there are bombing components in there that match the bomb that killed Judge Moran. You guys all know what you are looking for. You've done these bombers before, along with bomb factories, so be really careful on the evidence. We want to match it up if we can. We also have the computer forensics agent with us so any electronic devices we come across and seize under this warrant I want you to get them swept as quickly as possible. Get all other physical evidence to the laboratory in Atlanta and get that done as fast as we can. OK? Let's be safe and move forward."

The next morning the ATF Team including the Special Response Team assembled. They were in before dark around Miller's residence. They were watching through their night vision scopes and binoculars, they were in the woods, and they were in surveillance vehicles. They can see his house. No activity is reported by the surveillance team and they moved up stealthily to the front door. They announced their authority over a loud speaker, they breached the door with a ram, they yelled inside "Federal Agents with a search warrant, Federal Agents with a search warrant!" They heard no movement, there was no response, they waited for about a minute and a half to two minutes. They yelled again "Federal Agents with a search warrant!" There was no response. They slowly moved into the residence, they carefully looked for booby-traps and trip wires, anything that could be rigged with explosives. They checked each room and they found no one inside. Simultaneously, they were also searching the workshop in the rear where the welding equipment was seen. Within a matter of a few minutes, the tactical supervisor radioed back to Donnelly who was across the street. "Nobody is inside Boss. Now, we are having the explosives guys do a complete and thorough sweep looking for booby-traps before we do any searches for evidence."

Donnelly responded, "10-4. Got it, thanks Lou." Now the slow sweep for explosives and booby-traps began with ATF Explosive Enforcement Officers, certified Explosives Specialists and members of the Chattanooga Police Bomb Squad who've been called over to help. Along with the Tennessee Highway Patrol Bomb Squad who has also been called in for assistance. In a back bedroom, one of the ATF Certified Explosives Specialists noticed a small magnet switch on top of a dresser drawer. He stopped everybody and said, "This could be something here, let's move everybody out, get these bomb technicians to look at it." The agents were very suspicious of it, so they decided to take every precaution.

They used a small drill and a remote camera and went through the dresser drawer to view the inside without opening it. They looked up and saw that the drawer has been rigged from the inside with a trip wire with a magnet on the top. It was rigged to eight sticks of dynamite that were inside the drawer. If the drawer is opened the dynamite will explode. The Explosive Technology Branch's Explosives Enforcement Officer and a member of the Highway Patrol Bomb Squad then reached in with a specialized tool and they cut the string that's attached to the fusing and firing system for the bomb. They then safely opened the drawer, pulled the blasting cap out, which was the detonator to the dynamite and rendered the device safe. They radioed across to Donnelly and revealed, "We defused an improvised explosive device that was rigged with a trip wire in the dresser in the rear bedroom. That's all clear and we haven't found any other devices. "

Donnelly said, "10-4. Thanks very much." Donnelly asked for a report from the welding shop. They said, "Everything is clear of booby-traps boss. You can come on in." Donnelly walked across the street, he went into the house, looked around, Computer Forensics Agents were working on a laptop that was on a desk in a room next to the kitchen. Agents were taking photographs throughout the residence. Videotaping the action to show that the house was not damaged by the agents, and to also show the condition the house was the way it was when they entered. It was also for use in presentation in the court. Other agents were making a list of the items that were going to be seized for the back of the search warrant so they can return it to the Federal Judge. When Tim Donnelly entered Sparky Miller's house, he couldn't help but take note at how neat it was. There wasn't a thing out of place. Every piece of furniture was set perfectly. Every picture was straight, there was no dirt or grime on the floors. The kitchen was spotless, beds were made perfectly, everything was immaculate. It was a modest house but it looked freshly painted and was extremely neat. Being an ex-navy man, Donnelly was not surprised that he's a pretty meticulous guy. *He's very organized. He doesn't let things go to a mess. This is a guy that knows how to do things physically and gets them done. Surrounded by things in a straight line. Probably a little obsessive compulsive. An interesting bomber* thought Donnelly. The countertops were void of any superfluous knick-knacks. There weren't excessive pictures anywhere. Barely any really. There was a naval map of the North Carolina coast hung on one wall. There was a photograph of a welder with sparks flying that hung in the living room. Miller was proud of his skills as a welder and his service in the Navy as well. *Apparently, the Navy had taught him a lot* thought Donnelly. *How to be neat, how to live, how to work hard. This guy was no slouch. This is not the home of a lazy person. This was a person who was terribly busy in their life.* As Donnelly walked out the side door toward the workshop in the back, he noticed how neat everything was there as well. Even the outside was immaculate. There wasn't a thing out of place. Everything was as it should be. When he walked into the shop, again, neat toolbox, things arranged perfectly, hung on the wall. Not a mess anywhere. *No, this guy,* thought Donnelly, *he could make an awful plan. He's got the mind to do it. He would spend the time making sure every detail was right. Just like he does with his house, his yard and his workshop. This is not a man to fool around with.* It has numerous outbuildings, a couple of abandoned vehicles in the back of the workshop. Even the abandoned vehicles were placed meticulously and mowed around perfectly. They looked more like decorations than abandoned cars. A lot of steel and welding equipment was outside the workshop.

Donnelly walked over to the welding shop where his Explosives Specialists and Officers were inspecting things on the work bench.

Donnelly asked, "What have you got?"

Brenda answered, "It's a treasure trove of evidence boss, bomb factory for sure. Look at all these plates. Probably where he was welding the box to kill Judge Moran. Here's his soldering table with all the wires. Over here are the electric blasting caps that looks like Dupont. This guy is well prepared. We found some explosives out back. They were in a military ammunition box stored in a steel toolbox behind the shed. There is quite a bit of stuff."

Donnelly asked again, "What did he have?"

Brenda answered, "He had dynamite, he had a little bit of military TNT. It looks like stolen stuff. He even had a bag of ammo back there. This guy knew how to shoot it for sure, but his main skill was in fusing and firing. He knew how to set up those booby-traps and how to rig the remote-control."

Donnelly asked once more, "What about the remote-control transceivers? Did you find that?"

Brenda replied, "Yep, it's inside the shed and the servos are missing. All the stuff that was used in the Judge's bomb. We definitely can connect to this. We ought to get matches all over."

Donnelly said laughing, "Yeah, they'll be having a party at the lab with matching all this stuff."

Brenda responded, "Yeah those lab boys and girls get all tingly and excited when they can match this much stuff together."

Donnelly added, "OK, let's get it all bagged and tagged. Brenda, I want you to get this stuff down at the Atlanta ATF lab as quick as you can. Get it logged in, get it on the search warrant return. See if we can get some matches. Great work everybody, but now we have got to find Sparky Miller. Let's meet across the street and discuss that immediately." In a few minutes, Donnelly met with his supervisors and case agents across the street.

Donnelly said, "Well, it looks like we got the goods on him. Now, we've got to find him. Brenda, can you draw up the affidavit for a federal complaint and arrest warrant on Miller for the murder of Judge Moran with the bomb?"

Brenda replied, "Yes, Sir, I can."

Donnelly requested, "Alright, I need you to get on that as quick as you can. Let's get that complaint prepared and get the federal warrant signed. In the meantime, we got to do some heavy work to find Miller. Who has talked to the local police and the County Sheriff?"

Hightower says, "I talked to the sheriff. He doesn't have any new information but he has alerted all his deputies."

Donnelly, "Bill, do we have any possibilities on where he's at?"

Bill Hightower informed, "Well, we have a few leads, but so far, the ones we've checked haven't panned out. He drives a pickup truck with a camper. We have the description out to all the local police departments, deputies, and troopers in the area but so far nobody's picked up on him. The guy is kinda squirrely, he moves around a lot. The locals know him, he comes and goes and apparently, as we know it, he's been in Nashville on occasion. He could be here; he could be there or anywhere in between. He could be anywhere up in these mountains. You know how easy it is to hide out up here."

Donnelly replied, "Yeah, I sure do. If a guy doesn't want to be found, you can be sure he'll make it pretty difficult to do. That last fugitive we had that hid in these mountains; it took us two years to find him. I hope it doesn't get that drawn out. I want to get this guy wrapped up. He's extremely dangerous."

Chapter Eighteen:
The Stalker is Stalked

Donnelly assembled his team of agents and police officers at the ATF office in Chattanooga, Tennessee. The search warrant had been successful and the bomb factory uncovered. It was a bonanza of evidence. There was steel plate to match the steel plate in the bomb that killed the Judge. There was electric blasting caps and explosives that would match exactly to what was found by the laboratory in Judge Moran's bomb. There was a soldering table with wires and cutters where the device had been put together. There was even the box from the local Hobby Lobby where Miller had purchased the remote-control airplane and the transmitters. All of the evidence was clearly there to match Sparky Miller to the murder of Judge Moran. There was still a lot of pain staking work by the bomb technicians and explosive technology officers from the ATF and the forensics science laboratory personnel at the ATF office in Atlanta. The work had just begun but for Donnelly's team, all the answers they needed were right there.

However, the question that remained open was, where was the killer? Where was the bomber? Where was Sparky Miller? Could he have another bomb with him? Was he on a mission to hurt someone else? Did he know that ATF agents had searched his house? All these questions swirled around the meeting Donnelly was about to convene in Chattanooga. Donnelly's Assistant Special Agent in Charge, Valerie Johnson came in and said, "We have some leads, boss, on where Sparky Miller might have gone. Seems like he has a little cabin up in the mountains in Monteagle Tennessee and he would go up there to hunt and fish. We've talked to the sheriff up there in Grundy County and the police in Monteagle and also the Sheriff in Marion County and South Pittsburgh Police to see if we could get any leads on where he might be. We have intelligence that he has a cabin but so far, we have not been able to locate it. You know, that's a pretty vast mountain up there. Very difficult terrain and there are scores of cabins in those woods which makes it very tough. "

Donnelly said, "Alright, at least we have something to start with. Can we get our Technical Support Officers to do something with the cell phones? If we need a search warrant, Brenda will work on that with you to get some information from the phone company to locate his phone. If he's even carrying a cell phone. Does anyone know? "

Special Agent Brenda Humphrey who was the case agent spoke up, "Yes, we believe he has a cell phone, boss, but we just don't know if he has it with him or how much he uses it. He's kind of a quirky cat all around, so anything is possible with him."

Donnelly said, "Okay, well look, Valerie you got a team going up the mountain to see if they can coordinate with the sheriff and any troopers up there?"

Assistant Special Agent in Charge Valerie Johnson said, "Yes, Lieutenant Lopez from the Tennessee Highway Patrol is coordinating that."

Lieutenant Lopez said, "We can get air assets up there if you need them Mr. Donnelly. You know we have fixed wing and helicopters. We could bring them into the area if you want that sort of surveillances."

Donnelly remarked, "Thanks lieutenant, we might need it. The chopper may be something to scare him off but maybe a fixed wing surveillance could be helpful."

Lieutenant Lopez responded, "Okay, I will coordinate that with air support at headquarters and we will get a fixed wing down here close in case we need it."

Donnelly said, "Thanks lieutenant, that would be great."

Donnelly's worried. *Where's Miller? Could he be going to Nashville? Could he be after someone else he has a grudge with? Could he be after Tomi?* He wants to call Tomi, but everything they have done so far with the warrant, has not been public information. But he's worried about her.

He decided to make the call.

Tomi said, "Hello, Tomi Bardsley, Channel 4 news."

Donnelly replied, "Tomi, this is Tim."

Tomi said, "Hey Tim, where are you?"

Donnelly replied, "Well, I'm over in East Tennessee."

Tomi asked concerned, "What's going on? Does this have anything to do with the Judge Moran case?"

Donnelly answered, "It does."

Tomi asked again, "Do you have some leads? Is the story breaking?

Donnelly answered, "There are a lot of dynamics with it right now Tomi that we haven't released. It's getting real sticky. There is going to be some things breaking shortly, but the reason for my call is not news."

Tomi asked with a little shift in her tone, "Really, what is it?"

Donnelly answered, "It's your safety."

Tomi asked a bit worried, "My safety? Is the bomber coming after me?"

Donnelly said, "No, we don't know that. But we know who he is, we have served a search warrant on his property, we have the bomb making material."

Tomi said a bit relieved, "Oh Wow! I am going to break that story!"

Donnelly said, "Well, that's all I am going to give you Tomi. I think he probably knows that as well. I'm not going to give you his name right now but I am concerned that he could come over there, so I don't want you to go home. I am going to send an agent over to Channel 4 to be with you until we locate this guy."

Tomi responded, "OK! But I still want to report that there has been a break in the case."

Donnelly said, "Alright, I understand. Just be careful, watch your surroundings. We are going to locate this guy before he gets anywhere near you. We got some leads that he may still be in East Tennessee but we're just not sure of his whereabouts."

Tomi answered hurriedly, "Ok! Ok! Thanks Tim. I'll talk to you soon." Tomi rushed off to the editor to tell Lee about the break in the case she got from Tim Donnelly. Although it's not complete, it's still important information she wanted to get out there.

Donnelly was not concerned that the bomber knew they served a search warrant on his house. Everybody on the street and in the neighborhood knew they were there. It was such a big operation that it couldn't really be a secret. Miller was probably tipped off already by now by any number of people. Which is probably why he isn't around. So that wasn't of great concern to Donnelly. He was more concerned about Miller's whereabout. Donnelly released everybody and said, "OK, everybody to their tasks. Let's see if we can get some leads. Get some interviews going with some of these neighbors to try and get some tips. Get that team up in the mountain. Get the tech guys working on the phone. Brenda, get cracking on that arrest warrant, let's get going so we can get this guy." Brenda replied, "OK Boss."

About six hours later, Donnelly got a call from his Assistant Special Agent in Charge, Valerie Johnson.

Valerie said, "Boss, I think we got his truck located at a cabin up here on Monteagle Mountain. It's really rough terrain but I've got the Special Response Team surrounding it. Being exceptionally low key using their camouflage assets. They have a long rifle team watching the place. His truck is there. We think he is probably in there."

Donnelly said, "OK, good work. What else do you need?"

Valerie replied, "Well, we might need that fixed wing from the troopers closer just in case he rabbits on us. But right now, we think we can keep him in here. We are just on a waiting game at the moment. We haven't made any move on him yet."

Donnelly said, "Ok, 10-4. That sounds good. We might have a little time. Valerie, tell Bob to have Brenda get a telephonic complaint and warrant on Sparky Miller based on the evidence we found in his house. Have her explain that to the Magistrate Judge. We need a complaint here and we need a warrant signed as quick as we can. It will be good to have if we have to engage with this guy. We can do it either way but let's move to get that warrant."

Valerie said, "Ok, Boss."

Donnelly remarked, "I'll be leaving here shortly on my way up to the mountain."

Donnelly arrived on the mountain. He's with his team. It's past 11:00 pm. They met quietly down the road and the Assistant Special Agent in Charge briefed him. "All quiet. Tactical team thinks he's asleep. Nobody's moving in there now."

Donnelly said, "That's good. Let's just let him sleep. Maybe we'll move on him first light. Brenda has moved to get the Federal arrest warrant anyway. That will probably come in later. Let's plan on hitting him at 6:00 a.m. Pass that along to the SRT team."

The mountains of East Tennessee are steep, dense, and very lonely. People are scarce in these mountains and the weather is damp and cold. They don't carry the name "The Great Smokey Mountains" for nothing. There is always a misty fog that hangs in the air. The forest streams run like spaghetti strands down the mountains in all directions.

The rain clouds feed them constantly. Trekking through the brush can be very arduous and slow. People like Miller who know these woods can easily hide and not be seen. Miller's cabin was deep in the woods but still, the ATF agents were able to find it. You could almost hear Dueling Banjos playing in the background. Helped by the local deputy sheriff and state troopers, they were able to get around the cabin surreptitiously to watch Miller. Many years ago, when ATF agents were plying these hills looking for white liquor, also known as moonshine, one of the key injuries agents would face, besides violence from the bootleggers, was having eye injuries from the tree branches while they were moving through the woods at night. It was always a dangerous place. Slipping and falling off a rock ledge could be fatal. One could easily twist an ankle, break a leg or even get shot by someone you're looking for. In this case, they were after a bomber, a murderer, and a killer of a Judge. Someone who wouldn't hesitate to set a boobytrap or shoot with a rifle. The agents had to tread gingerly as they went through the forest to be able to surround Miller's cabin. But they were trained in these types of operations and were able to achieve it and get things set in place.

At dawn, the Special Response Team, which had surrounded the house has decided on a tactic they call surround and call. They succeeded in getting Sparky Miller cell phone number. They were going to dial him up at dawn. When dawn broke, the SRT leader told his Chief Negotiator to call into the house. Everybody was ready. The phone rang. Miller answered, "Yeah?"

The Negotiator said, "Mr. Miller, this is Special Agent Issa from the Bureau of Alcohol Tobacco and Firearms."

Miller replied, "You sonsabitches. I know who you are."

Agent Issa said, "Mr. Miller, we have a warrant for your arrest for the murder of Judge Moran in Nashville."

Miller replied, "You got nothing on me you bastards. I ain't done nothing."

Agent Issa responded, "Well, Mr. Miller you need to step outside and you can work that out in court. Not with us this morning."

Miller retorted, "I'll be sorting everything out right now big boy. I'm not going anywhere with you. You can go to hell and you need to get off my property."

Agent Issa replied, "Well, we can't do that Mr. Miller. We have a warrant, and you have to come with us. We have to take you to court. If you could just relax. No one wants to hurt you. Nobody's going to hurt you.

Just comply with our orders, get a lawyer come to court, fight the charges. If you're innocent you can hash that out in the court room."

Miller: "I'm not going to no federal kangaroo court run by the Zionist Occupational Government. You guys are all corrupt. You know you just make stuff up. I'm not going to go that way. That's not happening to me."

Agent Issa said again, "Now Mr. Miller, you need to relax. I understand you don't like the government. That's not a reason for you to get hurt."

Miller replied in a high voice tone, "I'll show you what hurt is."

In a couple minutes the door of the cabin flew open and Miller stepped out. He was holding a rifle in his hands and as he raised the rifle, a member of the ATF Special Response Team fired a long rifle shot from a 308-caliber sniper rifle. It hit Miller in his shoulder and knocked him down. He dropped the rifle, and he was severely wounded.

SRT Tactical Operators moved closer and shifted the gun away from Miller, they observed him for any bombs or explosive devices, but didn't see any. They called for an ATF Tactical Medic who was a part of the SRT. He came to treat Miller's wound. An ambulance was called which they had on stand-by down the road and Miller was transported to the local hospital where ATF would guard him. Donnelly talked to his commanders. He said, "Good work everyone. He was obviously raising that rifle to shoot.

He knew we were there. It looked like it was going to be a suicide by cop. Too bad for him. It looks like he is going to make it. It was just a shoulder shot. That was a great shot. Who made it?"

"Special Agent Billy Russell, sir."

Donnelly praised him, "Billy, good work, it looks like you sighted him right down the barrel.

Billy replied, "Yes sir. Right down Miller's own rifle barrel right to his shoulder."

Donnelly said, "Good work everyone. Now let's get the team in this cabin to see if there is any more evidence. Let the explosive tech guys go in first of course to make it safe."

Donnelly made a call to Tomi Bardsley in Nashville and said, "Tomi."

Tomi replied, "Tim, what's happening? The editor is going nuts over here. They want to know what the heck is happening. Nobody knows anything, they don't know where you are. They don't know who this bomber is. They don't know what's going on."

Donnelly said, "Alright Tomi, I'm going to give this to you and nobody else is going to have it. We served a search warrant at 459 Flower Avenue, South Pittsburgh Tennessee. We recovered numerous items of evidence related to the bombing of Judge Moran. All that we recovered will be listed on the search warrant return. We will file that return with the Federal Magistrate Judge in Nashville later today. So, you'll be able to get that to see what the evidence is from the court records. That will be public information."

Tomi said excitedly, "Wow! That's great. Did you catch the bomber?"

Donnelly replied, "We did, he wasn't home. We had to come up to Monteagle Mountain and found him in a cabin. He came out with a rifle; we shot him in the shoulder. He's wounded, he's in the hospital. He's been arrested and he's being charged with the murder of Judge Moran. We will be bringing him back to Nashville as soon as the Doctor's get through with him and say he can be transported."

Tomi said with so much excitement, "That is great, just great Tim! I'm going to break this story before anybody has it."

Donnelly responded, "OK Tomi. Everybody is going to have it pretty soon cause we're not going to hold it, but you've got it a few hours before the rest of them. Good Luck."

Tomi said, "Thanks Tim. I cannot wait to see you. Call me as soon as you get back."

Donnelly replied, "I will."

Chapter Nineteen:
Everybody Wants to Know

When Tim Donnelly returned from South Pittsburgh in East Tennessee and reached his Nashville Office, he called in his Public Information Officer Special Agent Al Fuller for a conversation.

Fuller said, "Boss, the press is clamoring for information on Miller. We got to get out there pretty soon."

Donnelly replied, "Yes, for sure Al, I understand. Let's do it first thing in the morning. Give them time to assemble. How about 10:00 am?"

Fuller responded, "Ten o'clock a.m. great boss. Where are we going to do it?"

Donnelly replied, "We can do it right here at the ATF office. Make sure you invite everybody; Chiefs, Sheriffs, Prosecutors, D.A. and the U.S. Attorney. Let's have it all right here. We'll announce the arrest, but let me check with the D.A. and the United States Attorney first and make sure it's okay with them. Let me make that call right now and I'll get back with you."

The district attorney and the U.S. Attorney agreed to hold the press meeting at the ATF office and the next morning at 10:00 a.m., all the law enforcement authorities arrived to hold the news conference. The U.S. attorney started it off with laying out the charges against Louis "Sparky" Miller in the bombing murder of Judge John Moran. He was followed by the D.A. All the law enforcement officials had great praise for the investigation and of course, they had already invited Judge Moran's family to be at the press conference. Tim Donnelly stepped up to the microphone to address all the reporters with Tomi Bardsley watching intently. Donnelly outlined the operations in Marion and Grundy Counties in East Tennessee. He described the search warrant at the residence of Louis "Sparky" Miller and the recovery of key evidence to be used against Miller that was listed on the back of the search warrant return which was public information. Donnelly then outlined the location where Miller was found in a mountain cabin, how it was surrounded, and how negotiators were called in. He talked about Miller's refusal to comply and to come out. How he eventually came out with a rifle and raised it toward the surrounding Special Agents, and then how one Special Agent fired a single round from a long rifle and hit Miller in the shoulder wounding him and affecting his arrest. Needless to say, the reporters were all excited about the end of this case regarding the bombing of a Judge. They were clamoring with questions about all aspects of the case.

Authorities were limited in what information they could provide. Yet, they tried to be as forthcoming as they could without jeopardizing the case. There were a few questions from reporters and then all the authorities filed out through the back door. As the press conference ended, Tomi Bardsley saw the ATF

Public Information Officer, Special Agent Fuller standing in the wings and she approached him and said, "Agent Fuller, is there anything else you can tell me besides what was given out at the press conference?"

Fuller replied, "I'm sorry Ms. Bardsley, you've got everything the boss has put out. There is nothing else that can be said right now. There will be an arraignment and a preliminary hearing of course in the courts and maybe there might be some more information you can gather at that time."

Tomi replied, "Okay, thank you so much, Agent Fuller, I really appreciate it. I guess Tim is pretty excited about making that arrest, huh?"

Fuller responded, "Well, I think he was excited until he got a phone call just prior to the press conference."

Tomi asked, "What phone call are you talking about?"

Fuller answered, "Oh, you didn't know, the boss got a phone call from Washington just before they walked out to give the press conference. He's been transferred."

Tomi asked surprised, "Transferred!? Transferred to where?"

Fuller answered, "Dallas Texas. He said he doesn't want to go. He argued with them but to no avail. You know being in the ATF is akin to being in the military. When they want to transfer you, you don't have a choice. They transfer the Agents in Charge a lot."

Tomi replied, "Oh My Gosh, I didn't know anything about this."

Fuller responded, "Well he is absolutely not thrilled about it at all."

Tomi said, "Well, thanks Agent Fuller. I'll see you later."

Tomi rushed out with her cameraman. They don't have a lot of time. They have to get to the station; they have to get this video tape of the news conference out. They have to make a package story for the noon and 5:00 p.m. news hours, and 6:00 p.m. and 10:00 p.m. as well. This is a big story and the Editor wants a lot of information on it. As they exited the ATF office, Tomi got in her news van with her cameraman, her phone rang. It was Tim. "Tomi, you got away before I had a chance to talk to you. I need to talk to you."

Tomi replied, "I'm rushing off to the station Tim, I have to get to work on the story for the upcoming news cycle. But I already heard your news."

Tim asked, "What news are you talking about?"

Tomi responded, "That you've been transferred to Dallas. Fuller filled me in."

Tim retorted, "Fuller needs to keep his mouth shut. I wanted to tell you this myself, Tomi. I thought I was going to see you in the hallway after the press conference but you were already gone when I looked out."

Tomi said, "Well, I am in such a rush to get this story out Tim. You know, it's a big news."

Tim replied, "I understand. But look, we have got to get together and talk. When are you going to be free?"

Tomi responded, "I've got to get back to the station and do two packages for the news tonight. But I'll be off about 6:00 and hand it off to the night crew. I should be free by 7:00 to get together."

Tim said, "Okay, Tomi, look, I'm going to pick you up at 7:00 p.m. I'm taking you out tonight, we're going to get something to eat and we are going to talk about this Dallas thing."

Tomi replied, "Yes, I'm pretty upset about it, Tim. I really would like to hear what's going on."

Tim responded, "Sure baby, I promise I will tell you all about it. I'll fill you in on everything. We're going to go down to Franklin. I know a couple of good spots we can hang out and just be together and talk about it."

Tomi replied, "Alright, I'll be ready. See you at 7:00 p.m."

At 7:00 p.m., Tim arrived at Tomi's house to take her out and discuss his transfer to Dallas in addition to the excitement over the arrest of Louie "Sparky" Miller. They kissed passionately in Tomi's front hall and she said, "I have just been worried about this all-afternoon, Tim. About you being transferred to Dallas. I don't know how this is all going to work for us."

Tim replied, "Don't worry Tomi, we are going to talk about it and try and work something out. Get your coat, let's go. The Uber is waiting." They jumped in the Uber, and headed down to the Harpeth Hotel in Franklin, Tennessee. As they exit the Uber, they walked between two large eight-foot-tall table lamps and an array of sconces lit by gas that graced the front door of the Harpeth Hotel. They walked inside the hotel together and noticed the thoroughly modern decor with the obligatory token guitar hanging on the wall. There was an open courtyard in the back with a small 3-wheel Cushman truck that served as the outside bar. They took a seat at the U-shaped bar. Tomi ordered a Stella and Tim got a Guinness, and they started to talk. The bar was quiet, 7:30 on a Thursday night, there's a few people lounging. It's a modern place trying too hard to be cool and Donnelly felt the place has already jumped the shark. Nevertheless, it's frequented by Country Music celebrities and famous people in the Franklin area and he wanted a quiet place to begin the evening. They had a few sips of beer and started discussing the matter at hand. Throughout the night, they were discussing their future together. After they finished their drinks, they walked a few blocks down by the Franklin square to go to another place called *Oh Be Joyful*. "Funny name for a bar" Tomi said as they walked in.

Tim responded, "Yeah, it sure is, it's a little hole in the wall but a cute place. It's a lot of fun. They play great music and I always like coming here. You can sit at a counter at the window, have a drink and people watch. It's a great place for conversation and tonight it will be just right. "Okay," Tomi said. As they walked in, they were lucky to get a couple of stools by the window, watching the passerby's walk down main street having a beer and talking quietly. They decided this was where they were going to have dinner. Tim ordered a burger and

Tomi ordered the wings. The orders came with the most delicious French fries Tomi has ever had. Their food came out hot and delicious. With such a busy day, neither of them had much time to eat and they devoured their meal. Again, they dived deeply into the issues that now plagued their future. *What was going to happen when Tim goes to Dallas? Are they going to be together? Can they date long distance? Are they still going to be an item?* All these questions were swirling around in Tomi's head. Tim was being extremely nice and sensitive. He kept touching her hand, while listening to her every concern but he was not totally saying what's going to happen. After another drink at *Oh Be Joyful,* Tim said, "You know Tomi, we need to get our mind off of this for a little while. Let's walk a few blocks from here to Kimbro's pickin' parlor. They have live music." So, they walked out to main street, went to the courthouse square, and turned east. They walked three blocks through a residential neighborhood. The street was lined with these beautiful big homes that had been there for probably over 150 years. Meticulously cared for, maintained and obviously loved. Strikes from musket balls could be seen in some of the houses in Franklin. As all these houses were there when the civil war was raging. At the famous Battle of Franklin, eight generals were killed as union and confederate forces clashed and battled for control of Tennessee. They walked down the sidewalk and turned down the street to go to Kimbro's. It's a small brown house, with a little porch out front. Sitting on the porch were three men playing guitars. One woman was sitting on a couch and was singing an old country song. *This place is really different,* Tomi thought. As they walked inside, they could hear loud music to the left, people milling all about. She could see there were different rooms to the house. Tim said, "Let's go back here in the back corner first." They took a right, walked up to a little bar and ordered a beer. There was a small room to the left of the bar.

In that room was an extremely talented blonde woman named Amber, she was playing blues on the piano. She was singing and playing at same time. A young man was playing the saxophone behind her and two fella's sitting on rickety old tables were playing guitars. One of the two men named John, had a grey ponytail spilling out from under a fedora. Always smiling, he had a commanding knowledge of music. He could play and sing any song. Both Amber and John smiled and waved at Donnelly as they walked in. Tomi said, "Oh My Gosh, do you literally know everybody?" Tim replied, "I'm forced to know bad people but I strive to know good people, and these are good people." Jammed in the small room, they were singing, clapping, and stomping their feet to the tunes of the blues Amber was playing. *What a crazy place,* thought Tomi. *This little bitty room with all these people.* "What's going on Tim?"

Tim responded, "Well, this is called the pickin' parlor and these are just local people and musicians who come in, pick up a guitar or they bring their own. They start singing and playing. They're just people who love music. I love coming here. Everyone is very down to earth, extremely nice. It's a great fun place and it's the way the vibe always is."

Tomi said, "You always seem to find the coolest places Tim. Everywhere you go."

Tim responded, "Well it's just part of being an Agent, I guess. During business I have to find all the uncool places so when I'm off duty I like to find the cool places."

Tomi replied, "Well, that's pretty neat."

"Let's go back here," said Tim. He took Tomi's hand and they walked through the bar, past the front door, through yet another bar and into a little larger room where a very lively band was playing. People were dancing, the band was loud, singing rock and roll songs and a completely different vibe that was going on 100 feet away. "Wow," said Tomi. "This place is really rocking."

Tim responded, "Yes, this place is always fun, but it's kind of loud right now. Let's walk out on the patio." They walked out to the patio. It was airy and nice. They took a seat on a bench next to a fire pit and they started to talk once again. Their conversation went back to what's going to happen to their future and Dallas.

After a few more beers and dancing, they headed back to Tim's house. Tomi had never been there before, so she was interested in his décor and how he kept his house. She knew it would be immaculate. You don't dress immaculate and then be a slob at home. She was right, Tim's house was not small. It wasn't gigantic either. It was fully furnished. It wasn't overly decorated with a lot of knick-knacks or trinkets or fluff. Good quality leather furniture. A large rug in a couple of the rooms. A huge map of Tennessee was hung in the dining room. The kitchen was spotless. All three bedrooms were fully furnished. All three bathrooms seemed well stocked. She was impressed but not surprised. Tim turned on the music, they sat on the couch, Tim wrapped his arms around Tomi and said nothing. He just held her, stroking her back. He was so disappointed that he was being transferred and he knew Tomi was too. As

Tomi sat wrapped up in Tim's arms, she couldn't help but shed a tear. She did it quietly so Tim wouldn't know or see. *What's going to happen?* Tennessee to Texas is too far for long distance especially with the career's they have. They sat quietly snuggled up together. Tim took Tomi's face and started to kiss her. He saw the tears. He hugged her tighter and told her everything was going to be alright. Tomi believed him. He wouldn't lie to her, she knew that. He took her hand and led her to his bedroom. It was a man's bedroom for sure. Nothing frilly or overdone. Queen sized bed made perfectly. As they entered the bedroom, Tim turned on a small nightlight, just enough light for them to see each other and to be able to look into each other's eyes. Tim started to unbutton Tomi's blouse. He slipped it off her shoulders. She was wearing the sexiest bra he has ever seen. It was pink but has black lace over the top. Pink straps. Three pink pearls in the very center. He undid her jeans and slid them down. The panties matched her bra. What an incredible sight. This fit, sexy woman in the sexiest underwear he has seen. He was already hard and it got even harder at the sight. Tomi returned the favor and unbuttoned Tim's shirt and jeans. She slid them down. She was kissing his chest. It was so strong and masculine; the strength of his arms, his narrow waist. His entire body electrified her every fiber and she couldn't wait to have him inside her. Tim removed her bra and panties; he slid down his boxer briefs. As they both stood there naked, Tim reached down and started massaging Tomi between her legs. He slowly found the opening and reacted at how wet she was. He was instantly overcome. Feeling her that wet, he knew it was for him. He slid a finger inside and she gasped. Tomi's knees buckled just a little bit. She reached down and started massaging Tim. Very lightly, gently, arousing him to a fever pitch. She went down on her knees and put him in her mouth. A little more every time. She knew this was driving Tim crazy. Tim pulled her to her feet, took her to the bed, and laid her down in the middle. As he kissed her, he opened her legs, slowly slid down her body and put her in his mouth. It was so sweet and wet. Tim couldn't get enough. He was so gentle. He moved slowly and intently on his mission. He could see and feel Tomi writhing in ecstasy. She grabbed his head to hold on. Tomi was trying to delay her orgasm and wait for Tim but he was having no part of it. Tomi couldn't hold it any longer. She exploded in such an intense orgasm that her whole body started to shudder. Tim didn't stop, he didn't leave. He continued ever so gently. Her body continued to tremble. Tim wanted to make sure Tomi was completely satisfied. He wouldn't stop until she told him to. Tomi's orgasm seemed to last forever. Her body seemed like it was convulsing. She was moaning, a low sound in her throat. Her legs moving up and down on the bed. Tim didn't stop. The feeling was so intense that it a seemed like even her hair was tingling. When she could no longer stand it, she cried out.

"OK Tim! OK! OK TIM!" Tim stopped. Tomi was exhausted, still quivering trying to catch her breath. Tim crawled up beside Tomi and held her while she recovered. He kissed her intently after which they laid there quietly holding each other. Tomi was so in love with this man, it made her heart ache. Tim, laying there holding Tomi thought. *How can I leave this woman behind? I don't want a life without her. We have to figure this out.* As Tomi recovered, Tim rolled over, climbed on top of her. She opened her legs and he slid in. She was still wet from her orgasm and he slid in with ease. She was so tight and wet, and Tim's hardness hadn't subsided. It didn't take long and Tim's orgasm exploded inside of Tomi. His hips moving rhythmically as he continued. Tomi wanted him to be as satisfied as she was, so she continued to move her own hips until he collapsed. Tim had never been so sexually charged before by any woman. EVER.

Neither of them wanting to move, they laid there for what seemed like an eternity. They finally got up, cleaned up, crawled under the covers and fell asleep in each other's arms. Both completely satisfied sexually and emotionally. Both thinking of the future. The next morning, Tim got up first and got coffee ready. He got out juice, eggs, bacon, and bagels. Tomi was up shortly after. They had coffee and shared small talk about their date last night while making breakfast. After breakfast they, went into the living room with more coffee.

Tim suggested, "Let's talk about Dallas."

Tomi replied, "What is there to talk about? You've been transferred and you're leaving."

Tim said, "I am not leaving tomorrow. I have 45 days to report. We have 45 days here to spend together."

Tomi responded, "Okay, 45 days. Then what?"

Tim added, "I have thought about this. You could come to Dallas with me."

Tomi asked shocked, "What? Wait, you want me to come to Dallas?" Tomi was stunned. She was not expecting that at all. "Tim, I have a job here."

Tim said, "Okay, well, they do have news in Dallas. You are such a great reporter and after the job you did on the Miller case, you will get snatched up immediately by a TV channel there."

Tomi, her head swirling said, "I don't know what to say. I was not expecting this at all. I'll have to think about it."

Tim responded, "Of course I understand. I did spring it on you out of the blue. I do realize you did just buy some new cowboy boots for Nashville. They certainly won't go to waste in Dallas."

Tomi smiled at Tim, leaned over and kissed him intently. They cheered with their coffee. The next 45 days would be exciting.

Louie "Sparky" Miller was booked into the Metropolitan jail in Nashville Tennessee on the charge of murder of Judge Moran. Miller loudly professed his innocence but the jury found him guilty. The Judge in the case sentenced Miller to the death penalty. He said, "The killing of a Judge struck at the lynch pin of our Democracy. If we allow Judges to be murdered, the keystone of what upholds everything in our nation would fall. The Judge felt that no light sentence would work in a case as heinous as a premeditated bombing and murder of a Judge. The Federal Prosecutors and the state D.A. had agreed to try Miller in the State Court since Judge Moran was a state Criminal Court Judge. He could have been tried for the bombing in the Federal Court as well. They worked together, they provided the ATF agents and all the forensics laboratory support that the Federal Government could provide and that resulted in a strong murder case against Louie "Sparky" Miller.

Miller was taken by Deputies of the Davidson County Sheriff's Department back to the Metro jail. His belongings were gathered up and he was taken outside and down to a van where he was taken to the Riverbend Maximum Security Prison in Nashville. The ride only took about twenty-five minutes. Miller was processed into the state penitentiary. Besides Riverbend being maximum security, it also housed death row. Miller didn't sleep that night. His plan had gone awry. He had not planned on being caught and charged with the murder of Judge Moran. He laid awake all night on his bunk going through every step of his case and how it went wrong.

In the morning, prior to breakfast, the corrections officer came to Miller's cell. He rapped loudly on the bars. "Miller, I have a note for you from the warden." "A reprieve?" Miller yelled. "Certainly not for you Miller. Here's the note." The corrections officer handed Miller the note from the warden. The note read, "Dear Mr. Miller, we regret to inform you that your brother Lonnie, who was assigned to the general population at the Riverbend Maximum Security Prison, killed himself. His body was found this morning hanging in his cell." Miller laid back down on his bunk, put both hands behind his head, looked straight up at the ceiling. The only person he ever loved and cared about in the whole world was Lonnie. Not one other human and now here we are at the same facility, under the same roof and one of us is dead. Lonnie was gone and Sparky had just been sentenced to death for the Murder of Judge Moran who had sentenced his brother to life in prison. *How ironic* Sparky thought, *Lonnie was sentenced to life but in the end, he still got death.*

Chapter Twenty:
The Henchman's Evil Apprentice
Ten Years Later

The warden and the corrections officer stood by as Miller was strapped to the gurney. Miller asked the warden if he could speak to him alone. The warden asked the lieutenant to leave and he stood there alone with Miller. Miller was laying on the gurney strapped down, about to meet his maker when he said to the warden, "Warden, there are some facts I want to tell you."

The warden responded, "Alright Miller, do you want your last words to be heard by the witnesses? We can turn on the microphone if you want to address the assembled crowd. You don't just have to tell me alone because right now the microphone is off."

Miller replied, "No, warden, I want to tell you this alone. I have other things I want to say to the crowd when the microphone is on."

The warden asked, "Alright then son, what is it?"

Miller replied, "Well, warden, I am the one who killed my brother's wife Jo-Sue. She was the rottenest bitch in the world, and she treated my brother just awful. I decided she had to leave this earth and I was the only one who could make that happen. I was going to kill Jo-Sue and frame someone else for the murder. Of course, my plan wasn't to get Lonnie charged for it. That was the bumbling detectives who wound up focusing on my brother because that bitch wrote my initials in blood and they assumed it was Lonnie."

The warden responded, "Well, Miller, you may be just telling me this trying to clear your brother's name here in your final moments."

Miller said, "I am trying to clear my brother's name and I'll prove it to you. Let me tell you what happened."

The warden said, "Alright, go on."

Miller began, "Well, I planned to kill her and frame someone else. Lonnie would be free of her and so would I. So, one night when I knew Lonnie was on his regular fishing trip with his brother-in-law in Florence Alabama, I snuck in the house with a spare key Lonnie had given me when they first moved in. I'm certain that Lonnie had forgotten all about the key. I had a knife on her and made her strip down. She started screaming at me, calling me a low life and how she hated me as much as she did Lonnie. I started slapping her around and gave her a bloody nose. She was such a nasty vile bitch. I took her to the basement, hog-tied her and put a gag in her mouth. I put her face down on the cold floor. I stood over her and placed a garrot around her neck and started lifting her up by the neck. Every time I pulled up on the garrot her own body weight was strangling her. But I didn't do it right away, I did it over and over and over until she was almost dead and then I would let her down again. She deserved every inch of it I'm telling you."

The warden replied, "Alright Miller, but that's not going to stop your execution."

Miller continued, "I know it's not, warden, I don't want to stop it anyway. I'm ready to go to hell. The plan was that I was going to frame another man for the murder of Jo-Sue and then me and Lonnie would be free of all this. But when those detectives charged Lonnie, I had to have a plan to see if I could get him out. The one standing in the way of any appeal Lonnie had was that rotten SOB Judge Moran. So, I took care of him. Of course, I wasn't planning on getting caught for that. But they never did make me out as the murderer of Jo-Sue. But then when my conviction of the bombing was announced, Lonnie hung himself in his prison cell.

Once I got that news there was no sense in revealing that I killed Jo-Sue because the whole purpose was to get Lonnie out, and here I was in prison for the bombing. By that time, it didn't do me any good to tell anyone about Jo-Sue. But now since it's all done, I can't help Lonnie and I can't get out of this rap. I guess I just got to take the deal that Satan dealt me. One of the best ways to finish all this, is to just let you and all the cops and feds know how I did it and what I did. At least this will clear Lonnie's name."

The warden responded, "Alright Miller. How do I know you are telling me the truth and not some bullshit story?"

Miller added, "Well, warden, you tell that fed Donnelly and those detectives, if they go behind my house in South Pittsburgh, there is a shed in the back. Five steps behind the northwest corner there is a white rock. I painted that rock myself. You lift up that rock, it weighs about ten pounds and dig a hole right there. Two feet down you are going to find a metal box. Inside the metal box is the garrot I strangled that bitch with, the K-bar knife along with the spare house key, the clown mask and an envelope. You'll find her DNA all over the place. You'll also find her clothes along with my shirt which has blood on it. I took them to cover any of my own DNA that might have ended up on them. You'll find the gloves I used and there is also a video recording on a thumb drive I made of me killing her. It's proof positive I am the killer. I kept it for the second part of my plan, the frame job. However, I was never able to get to that. With Lonnie gone at least I can use it to clear his name."

The warden responded, "Alright Miller, if it's any consolation to you I'll tell the feds and the detective what you told me. Maybe we can go and retrieve that stuff. It doesn't make much difference now. Jo-Sue is dead, Lonnie is dead, the Judge is dead and in a few minutes you'll be dead."

Miller said, "That's right warden. I am anxious to go. There is nothing left for me in this world." The warden turned and signaled to the lieutenant to open the door. Just then the warden stopped. "Wait a minute Miller," he said. "You didn't say who you were going to frame for Jo-Sue's murder.

Miller said, "Well, warden, that changed after Lonnie was convicted. My original plan was to frame an old Chief Petty Officer that I hated from the Navy. You know I loved my brother Lonnie more than anything in this entire world."

The warden replied, "Well, I knew your brother Miller; I was the warden when they first brought him in."

Miller responded, "I know warden, I saw your name above the door in giant letters every time I visited Lonnie. It's burned in my memory. You bear part of the responsibility for keeping an innocent man in prison."

The warden said, "Come on Miller, you know I have no control over who is sent to my prison."

Miller replied, "Everybody has a little control, the detectives, the Feds, the jury, The D.A., the attorneys, the Judge, even you warden. But nobody has the guts to step up, speak up, and right the wrong. You all have dirty little hands as far as I am concerned."

The warden responded, "Well, son you bear the most responsibility because you killed your brother's wife."

Miller said, "That's different, that had to be done."

The warden sought, "Alright son. Go on, so who were you going to frame?"

Miller answered, "Everyone and no one. I wrote the name on a piece of paper and put it in an envelope. It's in the box with the other evidence. Do me a favor warden, when you get the envelope, will you call the guy and tell him what a lucky bastard he is."

The warden replied, "Alright Miller."

Miller said, "Well, that finishes it I guess, I will see you in Hell, warden."

The warden retorted, "I don't think so Miller, I have other plans."

Miller said, "Your plans may not work out the way you hope warden, the devil's breath may still reach you, after all, every dog has his day. Today may belong to your puppet government but tomorrow and forever belong to me.

The warden replied, "That may be true Miller, but today is definitely not your day, and you have no tomorrows."

The warden walked out of the death chamber. The microphone was then turned on for the assembled crowd.

When all was said and done, the warden called the sheriff of Marion County. He gave the sheriff all the information he got from Sparky Miller. The sheriff was very aware of "Sparky" Miller from the bombing investigation 10 years ago.

The sheriff said, "Thanks warden, I'll get my detectives and call TBI with their evidence technician and I'll notify Metro Nashville Homicide and ATF. We'll need a search warrant but that should be no problem with all you've told me."

The sheriff, the Marion County Sheriffs' detectives, three TBI Agents, two ATF agents from the Chattanooga office, two Metro Nashville homicide detectives, TBI forensics evidence technicians and a half a dozen sheriff's patrol cars all descended like a swarm of locusts on the Miller house which was just outside the city limits of South Pittsburgh. With the warrant in hand, the sheriff had already briefed the team. The warrant will lead them directly to the white rock behind the shed.

The sheriff instructed, "We're not searching the house or the shed. We are here to only dig up the white rock. There could be more evidence in the house and that is another warrant if needed. For right now we are limited based on this warrant to see what we can find."

The sheriff led the team in. TBI forensics team did the digging as everybody stood by. They dug two feet under the white rock. Sure, enough there was a metal box. Inside was exactly what Miller told the warden. The garrot made of parachute cord, women's clothing ripped and bloody, a knife, gloves, a man's shirt assumed to be Miller's, a clown mask, an envelope and the thumb drive with a video of the murder.

TBI agent confirmed, "Everything is here, exactly as described."

The sheriff replied, "Bag it and tag it. List it on the search warrant return and take it back to the Judge."

The team discussed this new evidence and how it would clear Lonnie Miller's name. The Metro Nashville homicide detective said, "Well it's proof positive we charged the wrong man. I'll get with the DA to discuss the findings to clear Lonnie Miller's name and to make a motion to the court to get the record of Lonnie Miller's conviction expunged."

The sheriff replied, "Well, it's the right thing to do, to clear his name. But since he's as dead as Jimmy Hoffa, he's never going to get a chance to realize it. I've got to call the warden back." The sheriff called and briefed the warden on what they found and to confirm Miller was telling the truth.

The warden said, "Thank you for letting me know. Sheriff, did you open the envelope you found inside the box? Miller told me he wrote the name of the person he was going to frame for the murder of Jo-Sue inside."

The sheriff replied, "Yes, we did warden. Do you want me to read it to you, because you are not going to believe it."

The warden said enthusiastically, "Yes, read it."

The sheriff said, "Warden Larry Mankowski. Riverbend Maximum Security Prison, Nashville. Along with your home address in Brentwood." The warden was silent for several moments trying to absorb what he just heard.

The sheriff added, "Warden? Are you still there?"

The warden replied, "I guess I'm the lucky bastard after all. Thanks sheriff."

The warden hung up and sat down in his green leather chair and thought about the injustice of an innocent man rotting and dying in jail for a crime he didn't commit. He thought about if Miller could have actually pulled it off and later framed him for Jo-Sue's murder. His head swirled with the intricacies of that plot. Being a warden in a Maximum-Security Prison, Warden Mankowski had been threatened many times. Threats came from inside the prison and also outside the prison. As a warden, you have to put your emotions aside and not get wrapped up in the menagerie of different personalities of the prison population. But that didn't stop his thought process, trying to understand if anyone like Miller, could actually pervert the justice system enough to be able to fraudulently get him charged with murder.

The warden's thoughts then spun back to Lonnie Miller and his needless death. The warden spent his life as a Paladin for justice. He kept dangerous men locked up. But when the system goes this wrong it pained him deeply. He wished he could right the wrong but the bell had already tolled for Lonnie Miller. It has been a long couple of days for the warden. Last night at 6:00 p.m., Miller was executed and today the sheriff had served a warrant and discovered the evidence hidden in the box behind Miller's house. It was evening and the warden was tired. He left the prison for his 45-minute drive to his home in the upscale Nashville suburb of Brentwood. The warden's thoughts now changed to fishing, his favorite past-time. It's how he relaxed and got his mind away from the often-heavy burden of his duties. The warden's responsibilities were sometimes a Sisyphean task and the boulder had just rolled back down the hill and he needed a break. He arrived home and his wife Susan met him at the front door. She gave him a big hug and said, "Larry you look exhausted." As they walked inside, the warden said, "Susan, I need to get away. What do you say we go to Florida next week and do some fishing?" Susan replied, "Sounds great. Let's go in the kitchen and make a drink." As they walked into the kitchen, Susan pointed to a small package on the table and said, "This came for you today, looks like fishing gear." "Perfect," the warden said. "Let's hope it's some new lures and tackle." As Susan started to make the drinks, the warden began to open the box. He said, "Susan I feel very lucky that the condemned inmate Miller never got a chance to try to frame me. Not sure if it would have worked but nonetheless it would have been very stressful. "Yes," she replied, "I agree but he is gone now and he won't be able to do anything, ever."

The warden will never have to roll the Sisyphean rock up the hill again because at that exact millisecond, the bomb in the package detonated with a crushing blast that eviscerated the warden and sent Susan slamming into the wall behind her. She was embedded and hanging forward like a puppet with its strings cut. She was bleeding from devastating wounds and died instantaneously. The warden was no more. Much of the warden's body was mangled in a sickening heap and smashed without mercy against the walls and stuck to the ceiling. His flesh clings to every crevice in the kitchen appearing to have been put through a giant shredder. It was a scene of unimaginable horror. The blast was heard for many blocks in the quiet neighborhood. It set off the fire alarm in the house and the kitchen caught on fire. Smoke was pouring from the structure when the homes National Certified Alarms (NCA) triggered and called 911. Neighbors who heard the blast and saw the smoke also flooded 911 with calls.

The bomb turned the kitchen into a crucible of fire and heat, unforgiving steel shards were omnipresent and smoke billowed from the windows announcing the horrible crime. The blowing curtains whispered sweet revenge, there was no screaming, no moaning from the victims, only Lucifer's breath filled the air. A criminal bomb was a malevolent creature, the spawn of hell, it carried no kindness, it was never tender nor lamblike. It was designed only to launch the hated into eternity and snuff out life in a welter of blood and misery. Once its job was done, it never speaks again, it transmogrifies into everlasting silence. Fire fighters and police quickly arrived and doused the flames and discovered the gruesome scene. Brentwood police called for their detectives and ATF. They met on the scene and began an hours long crime scene process and investigation. Once detectives and Special Agents learned that a warden had been killed, they notified TBI and asked for their assistance. The FBI was also called in. The ATF Special Agent in Charge of the Nashville Division was Dana Flobe. Dana met with the Chief of the Brentwood Police and the director of the TBI and the Special Agent in Charge of the FBI. She said, "We're going to have a briefing in a few minutes from the agents processing the scene and conducting the investigation." Shortly, the team came in and was composed of Brentwood detectives, ATF, TBI and FBI. A Brentwood detective started the briefing and said the victims were Warden Larry Mankowski and his wife Susan. No one else lived in the house. They have a daughter that lives in Black Earth, Wisconsin. They have talked to the Police Chief of Black Earth Mitch Hogan and he had his officers complete the death notification. We're conducting a neighborhood canvas to develop any witnesses. Then the TBI Supervisor said that the TBI was just starting to conduct interviews with all the employees of the Riverbend Maximum Security Prison and was pulling the warden's personnel files. The ATF Supervisor told the commanders that the device looked to be a parcel bomb that denotated on the kitchen table. Most likely when it was being opened. It was a small rectangular metal box welded together. It had an electrical fusing and firing system that had nails and ball bearings added as fragmentation. The device blew a hole in the kitchen table and through the kitchen floor. It was a powerful blast and we are estimating three to five pounds of explosives. We can't tell for sure what kind of explosives were used until the ATF laboratory runs the tests on our submitted swabs. With the ensuing fire there was a strong possibility it was military grade explosives like C4 or TNT because they both have large flame fronts. Special Agent in Charge Dana Flobe then asked the ATF Supervisor if there was anything else that he has to report. He said, "Some of the Senior Special Agents are seeing similarities to a bomb we had 10 years ago that killed a Judge. We are pulling all the files now. One more thing, it appears that on one piece of a metal plate that was part of the box, the letters "LM" were engraved in the steel." The Special Agent in Charge commented, "I recall that bombing when the Judge was killed, I was assigned in Miami then. Wasn't Tim Donnelly the SAC at that time?" The Supervisor replied, "Yes, it was Mr. Donnelly." The SAC thanked everyone and stepped outside from the meeting and called her colleague, Tim Donnelly who was now assigned to Washington, D.C. "Hi Tim, it's Dana Flobe from Nashville."

Tim says; Hi Dana, can you give me a second. I've got Tomi on the other line."

Dana responds; "Sure I can wait."

Tim returns to Tomi, "hey baby what's going on?"

Tomi says; "You got a package today. Don't worry, I know the rules. I left it on the front porch for you.

Tim says; "I didn't order anything. Does it say where the package is from?

Tomi replies; The return address says Diablo Enterprises, LLC.

Tim responds; "I don't recognize that but I'll deal with it when I get home.

Tomi asks; "What time do you think you'll be home for dinner?"

Tim; "I'll be home around 8:00 p.m. I love you."

Tim gets back on the line with Dana and she described the situation to Donnelly. The bombing murder of the warden and his wife, the metal box and the letters "LM" engraved in the steel.

Donnelly paused for more than a moment and then he said, "Dana, the bomber in Judge Moran's case was the evilest characters I think that I have ever come across. I swear he was one of the Devil's Henchmen." He then paused and said,

"Did you hear about Louie Miller?"

READERS MATTER!

We would like to thank you for purchasing and reading our first book. We are fans of crime and romance as well. If you would be so kind as to take a minute or two and review our book on Amazon, we would greatly appreciate it. Reviews help both authors and new readers.

Thanks again.

Tami and Jim

Made in the USA
Middletown, DE
03 October 2023